AVA CUVAY

TIN TOY

"Tin Toy"

written by Ava Cuvay

Copyright ©2022

Published by Drinking the Stars Press, LLC

Cover Design by Fiona Jayde Media

Copy Edited by Nan Reinhardt

ISBN # 978-1-7334827-9-0 (print)

ISBN # 979-8-9871763-0-6 (digital)

Website: AvaCuvay.com

Facebook Page: AvaCuvayAuthor

✿ Created with Vellum

Dedication

To all Librarians and their many super powers.
To anyone who has hidden their true selves away just to survive.

Acknowledgements

Thank you to my Alpha Reader, Kelly Best-First-Fan-Ever Snyder with Twinsie Talk. Thank you for your input and suggestions on this story. And for loving Betty as much as I do!

Thank you to my fellow Hoosier Trips: Cindy Tanner and Melanie Jayne. Your support, encouragement, and camaraderie are priceless. You know exactly what to say when I need to hear it!

Chapter One

Betty Hayworth leaned back against the tufted cushion of the library loveseat, a holo-book clutched to her chest as she reveled in the emotional satisfaction of the twenty-first century historical romance she'd just finished. She hadn't understood much of the period slang—the antagonist had been *sus,* the couple had been *shipped,* the adventure *YOLO'd,* and all manner of items *yeeted*—but that had not lessened her enjoyment.

As if to prove her own point, a contented sigh escaped her lips.

She loved books, a passion supported by her job as director of a small neighborhood library in the eclectic, upscale Greater Broad Ripple area of Indianapolis, Indiana. She especially loved romance novels. Genre didn't matter; she read them all. Small towns, big cities, Regency England, even futuristic space opera. As long as the hero realized he wanted the heroine more than power, wealth, prestige, vengeance, or the family farm. As long as he vowed to stand beside her no matter life threw at them.

That's what she loved about romance novels. Passionate kisses. Hot sex. A swoon-worthy love interest.

And a happily-ever-after.

Because in this day and age, finding happily-ever-after was a real challenge for many individuals, most especially cybernetic individuals like her. Depression. Suicide. Glitches. Angry mobs of terrified citizens. Society in the twenty-second century tolerated cyborgs and cybernetic sympathizers about as much as Salem in the 1600s had liked witches.

Therefore, a vital ingredient to achieve her own happily-ever-after was not being outed as a cyborg.

Which made family, friends, and romantic relationships oddly detrimental to a happily-ever-after goal. Even for a happy-for-now goal.

Fortunately, Betty didn't have any of those detriments. Also fortunately, she didn't need them. Except for the rare occasion when she longed for human interaction more meaningful than recommending books to her library patrons, she had ready access to millions of characters who filled that void in her life. And not risk her own life in the process.

"Thank the Maker I love to read." She murmured into the quiet coziness of her neighborhood library, then glanced at the holo-book still in her hands. The *rom-com* story and its bumbling hero still circled around her brain and gripped her heart. "Otherwise, I wouldn't have you to add to my ever-growing list of book boyfriends, Mr. Tall-Dark-and-Social-Media-Influencer… whatever that is."

Betty uncurled from the cozy loveseat and slipped into her leopard print pumps with the red bows. She left her empty teacup on the side table and returned the book to the stack of new arrivals she'd received yesterday. One caught her eye and punched her gut in unison. The latest from a popular author of political cyborg thrillers, a regular patron had requested it. Otherwise, Betty wouldn't have ordered it. Ever. Society hated cyborgs enough as it was, she didn't need to feed into the ugly stereotype of them as unhinged psychopaths or emotionless killing machines.

Yet, she held a book depicting cyborgs in that exact manner.

Unlike the *futuristic* romance books from the previous century, today's authors never painted cyborgs as the heroes or the love interests. They were the villains, and the villains always lost in the end.

She'd personally lived that particular truth for the past several years and didn't need the reminder stacked among the library's shelves. Didn't want to face those patrons who checked out the book—a book she admittedly judged by its horrid cover featuring a mangled cyborg—nor listen to those patrons talk about how wonderful the book was or how realistic the cybernetic antagonist.

"You might have to suffer an irreparable injury." She glared at the holo-book and shoved it to the side, battling a twinge of guilt for the threat. Taking her frustration out on library property would not change the world's opinion about cyborgs. Destroying the book wouldn't even hinder the author from writing another unpalatable cyborg-villain story. And her threat smacked of narrow-minded censorship, like the book burnings of centuries past. Freedom of opinion, the open exchange of ideas, was integral to her role as a librarian. She was the first line of defense against the tyranny of the thought police, the keeper of free speech. It was her superpower.

A superpower which conflicted with her secret existence as a public pariah.

She glanced around the homey little library which had once been someone's quaint two-story house complete with gingerbread trim and a white picket fence. Second-hand ottomans and tufted armchairs scattered amid floor-to-ceiling bookshelves. The murals painted on the front bay windows colored what little light they allowed inside, lending a dance-club vibe to the room. No, wrong imagery. The streams of rich rainbow hues, catching on the particles of floating dust, were more akin to the reverence of a church, especially in the muted quiet which accompanied it. Her own little oasis amid the noise of the city outside these walls. A tranquil refuge for the weary, wandering soul looking for respite. A gateway to thousands of worlds a person could explore from the safety and comfort of a cozy loveseat and cup of Earl Grey.

She rubbed her temples, the silence of the library a banging gong in her head. As much as she appreciated her quiet existence, maybe the monotony wore on her. A wistful thread of desire for friendly conversation with someone who wasn't a fictional character from a book wound through her heart. And a wave of desire for some interaction of a more physical nature wound through needier body parts, thanks in part to her recently enjoyed book. Family, friends, and romantic relationships might be detrimental to her safety as a cyborg, but she was still mostly human, and humans were social animals.

Other than the visit last week from the long-legged woman named Eve—the one who'd merely surfed the internet on the library computers and then raced out without a single good-bye, thank-you, or go to hell—Betty hadn't had a patron in weeks. And she hadn't been laid in years.

Loneliness reared its ugly mug on occasion, but such was a necessary side-effect of her plan: lay low and don't draw attention.

She snorted at the last bit. As if her pinup model couture from a bygone era could go unnoticed. Clothes emphasizing her curves and colors popping with knowing innocence, her appearance screamed *va-va-voom!* And her resting bitch face countered with *back off.* A nice balance, if anyone cared for her opinion, because it kept her safe, if a bit lonely and horny. But her appearance did not say *nothing to see here.*

On the up side, neither did it say *hey, I'm a cyborg.* Which was the crucial aspect of her *don't die* plan. She worked hard to keep her particular secret... well, a secret. If she was ever discovered, loneliness and forced celibacy would be the least of her worries.

The bell above the front door chimed its cheerful welcome to an incoming customer. Betty hastened around the desk to the front of the building, nearly giddy to have someone to talk to and a distraction for her churning internal thoughts.

A young man stood at the front. A stocky twenty-something wearing trendy jeans and a concert tee, he smelled like automotive lubricant and yesterday's bar tab. His belligerent expression seemed odd for someone who entered a library of his own free will, but she recognized him as a result.

"Welcome to the Greater Broad Ripple Public Library. I'm Betty." She greeted him, pasting a bright smile on her face even though her gut clenched. At least this was an ice bath to the simmering arousal the romance novel had kindled. "You came to the poetry reading last month, didn't you? Paul, right?"

He'd been an asshole then. His expression bespoke the fact he would likely be an asshole again.

He shoved his fists into his front pockets and glared at her with eyes bleary and bloodshot. Come to think of it, he'd been similarly inebriated at the poetry reading. "Yeah. My girlfriend dragged me. Said it would be *romantic*"—that word spoken as if it was a slimy bug—"but it was just a bunch of women reading about their fucking periods and how men suck."

True, there had been some of that, but she wasn't about to encourage his attitude. She shrugged. "It was an open mic evening. Participants read the poetry which spoke to them. I'm sorry you didn't enjoy the selections they chose."

"Didn't go thinking I'd enjoy it. I went thinking it would get me laid. Instead, my girlfriend bitched at me until I'd had enough and dumped her ass."

He'd accompanied a sweet, petite blonde who'd chosen a

touching poem about the patience and absolution of love. While Betty couldn't judge how a person might act in a private setting, the young woman had not seemed the bitching type.

Still, Paul looked at Betty as if expecting a reaction to his crass words. She shrugged. "Um, congratulations?" Honestly, where was this conversation headed and why were they having it?

"The opposite. I work for her dad, and he fired me. Said it was because I was a drunk, but I know it's 'cuz she cried to him about me being a shitty boyfriend." Paul glared at the side room where the poetry reading had been stationed. "Shitty boyfriend, ha. I treated her good. She just doesn't like me drinking. Doesn't understand that I'm relaxing. I like to play hard when I'm not working."

"Well, I'm very sorry for your troubles." No, she wasn't. She walked to the front door and grasped the handle, turning back to address him. "But, this is a library. Not an AA meeting, dating resource, or staffing agency. I'm afraid we have nothing here to offer you."

Not true. The library had plenty of resources available for him to propel himself into a new career, relationship, or sobriety. She didn't even need to reference her CPU's body language database for proof he wanted a scapegoat, not a solution, so she opened the door and tilted her head toward it, clearly indicating he should leave.

He didn't.

Instead, he sauntered toward her, his gaze roving her from head to toe and all her assets in between as if he approved. As if she could rest easy now, assured she had acquired his endorsement. He licked his lips like she was a tasty morsel. She swallowed the groan and managed to refrain from rolling her eyes. Did he think that was sexy? Did he expect her to giggle, flip her hair, and yowl like a cat in heat?

The art of seduction was wasted on the young and inebriated.

He stopped in front of her, his whiskey breath wilting her pin curls and his eyes squarely focused on her chest. She wore a cropped cardigan over a boat-neck top, so there was no visible cleavage. However, short of wearing a cardboard box, she couldn't hide the ample curve of her breasts and he assumed that was an invitation to leer. "Nothing to offer me, huh? This is a library, and I'd like to check you out."

Her derisive snort came before she could stop it. She might be horny, but she wasn't desperate. Grateful the thought didn't rush out of her mouth like the snort had, she plunked a hand on a hip, and leaned on the door, her words clipped. "May-December romance tropes are out of favor at the moment. But if you're looking for reading materials, I'd recommend craft books on how to be more than a one-dimensional character. Or psychology books on what women want from a man, and—trust me—it's not to be ogled. These can all be checked out for two weeks with a valid local ID. But as for me, I just work here."

She flashed him her biggest *get-lost* smile and waved toward the outside.

Instead of taking the not-so-subtle hint, he blinked a few times while her words soaked into his 80-proof gray matter. He scowled. All the anger over his own inept life directed at her as if she was the cause for his woes. His hands fisted at his side. He tensed, ready to lunge at her, and growled. "Look here, you b—"

Betty stepped away, pretended to wobble and lose her balance, then slammed the edge of the door into his face. "Oh, heavens! I am so clumsy!" She feigned surprise and concern. Blood spurted from his nose and dribbled on his shirt before he could cover it with a hand or curse at her. She reached for him— "Goodness, let me help you with that."—and shoved him outside, then closed and locked the door.

"You want me to call an ambulance?" She yelled through the

wood door. Without waiting for a response, she walked back to the kitchen to brew another cup of tea. Hibiscus this time, to celebrate. She might be a librarian, but her real superpower was ousting assholes.

Chapter Two

"You want me to *what?*" Everett Dean gawked at the man seated next to him in the cockpit of the twin engine jet, expecting to see two heads. Antony, his normally sensible personal pilot and bodyguard currently spouted words which would make even the most outlier conspiracy theorist blink.

"I want you to change out of your business suit. Secure the *bugout bag* I packed for you, then put on that parachute, Boss."

"This is a business trip, Antony, not a pleasure jaunt. I will not jump out of a perfectly good airplane, especially at night. The joke's not funny."

"You know I don't joke." Antony shook his head. "'S not my style."

Everett knew it. "If something's wrong with the plane, turn back to O'Hare. I'll reschedule with Director Hawks."

The corporate jet was at thirteen thousand feet and climbing, headed to D.C. for Everett's meeting with the director of the Department of Cybernetic Oversight and discuss possible terrorist sabotage of the cyborg industry. Weather was clear from here to the East Coast and Antony had flown the route so many times, he could probably do it in his sleep. So why would tonight's trip be so special the former airman had packed a small duffel filled with emergency provisions for Everett? And why hadn't Antony packed one for himself?

Antony glanced at him, his expression as somber as ever. Perhaps even more so. "The plane's fine, Boss. And maybe nuthin's gonna happen. I just… I gotta feeling 's all. You ever get a feeling?"

"Not one I trust. You know I follow my brain, not my gut."

Prior to this week, Everett might have laughed Antony's words away. But not now. Not after clear evidence the man might have a point. Everett's meeting with the DCO was because he'd found a virus on his personal company network. A virus which didn't wipe out the corporate mainframe or siphon company funds to a secret Bahamian bank account, either of which would have been preferable to its true function. This virus had sent out global communications containing so-called proof that Preditech—the company Everett had built with unerring vision into the foremost authority on cutting-edge cybernetic technology—had a fatal flaw in their implant systems which they chose to ignore rather than fix because they were greedy capitalist bastards.

The accusation rankled because why the fuck was it so wrong to make money? And because it wasn't true.

Antony stared out the windshield into the darkness dotted with signs of civilization receding beneath them. "Wacky shit's going on, Boss. I'm being cautious because the X-factor doesn't give me warm fuzzies. In your bugout bag is a handheld oxygen can with a mask. Keep that out and ready in case cabin pressure drops. This jet has an over-wing escape door you open from the inside. Make sure you jump clear."

"You're not making sense. Turn back. I'll reschedule the damn meeting and we'll figure this all out." Everett ground his molars. This was a *Twilight Zone* episode. Or horror movie. And he was more a documentary kind of guy.

Antony checked a dial with the same calm confidence he always had. He looked at Everett, the dull red shadow glowing in his cybernetic eyes, his face as serious as a heart attack. "All the shit happening lately, it's about cyborgs, right?"

He meant the strange string of recent incidents. First the virus. Then the disappearance of Preditech's accounting exec, Eve Myer, after she'd downloaded a copy of the virus. Then her death in an apartment fire which left nothing of that Chicago brownstone building except bricks and ash. Then a suspicious ping to her company email account by an unauthorized IP address the day after she died.

Then the final nail in the coffin: the cyborg who had turned rogue and brought Chicago's Sunday rush hour to a standstill while he systematically destroyed everything in his wake until the police finally gunned him down... ten feet from Everett's town car.

Everett cleared his throat. "Cyborgs? I think it's a stretch to say that—"

"Okay, maybe not cyborgs. But it's definitely about you."

"You're just being paranoid."

"That's my job. And maybe you should be paranoid, too. Look Boss, I'm a cyborg, 'member? Which makes me an X-factor. What happens if I go rogue and bury this plane in the ground with you in it?"

"Assuming it isn't a rhetorical question, we both die." Everett obliged the pilot's question. He paid Antony to be cautious about safety and potential threats. But how had the man connected the events and come to such a conclusion? Everett sighed in frustration. "But you know as well as I do the number of cybernetic individuals who *go rogue* is statistically insignificant. It's Hollywood and a bored news media making a big deal out of it. We don't even know why cyborgs go rogue—"

"Right, we don't know. And it only takes one rogue cyborg to end your life. A cyborg like me—"

"You planning on going rogue?" He shot back, irritated with Antony's tenacity on the topic. Unease churned Everett's stomach. Or maybe his dinner salad had contained tainted lettuce. "Antony, if I'd spent my life afraid someone might want to kill me, I never would have left my laboratory, much less forged Preditech into the company it is today."

"You also got where you are by bein' smart. And a smart man should put the dots together." Antony snapped at him, his tone out of character yet stopping shy of calling Everett a dumbass. Antony huffed. "Boss, d'you ever wonder why cyborgs *go rogue*? Imma glorified computer. If someone can plant a virus on your company computer, what's to say they can't put a virus in me and overpower my control of my own parts?"

Everett had designed the company network himself—child's play after his breakthrough in synthetic-to-organic cybernetic systems integration—and the network was failsafe, completely unhackable. Until someone had hacked it. An untraceable source had hacked his fucking network and plopped a damn virus down in the middle of it. If his network had been hacked, he had to at least admit the possibility cybernetic systems could also be hacked no matter how encrypted their systems were when they left Preditech's factory.

"Look. Even if we turn back or nothing happens tonight, that don't mean you're safe." Antony sighed. "You need to watch your six, Boss. I got a bad feeling about this."

"I take it you're not talking heartburn." Everett tried to lighten the ominous mood which filled the cockpit. On business flights, he liked to sit with Antony, who droned for days about airplane mechanics and flight history, but it made for better conversation than the profit/loss statements awaiting his review. Although tonight's conversation didn't exactly qualify as *better*.

Antony gazed out at the dark night sky as their arcing path swooped them over northern Indiana. One hand operated the yoke with casual skill. The other hand rested on the instrument panel, the slender data probe from his cybernetic hand extending out his forefinger and into a port for instantaneous information exchange. "Just humor me, boss. If I'm wrong, I'll buy you a beer and you can laugh at me."

Everett loosened his tie and scrubbed a palm along his jaw's five-o'clock shadow, shaking his head at the strange direction the evening had taken. After several quiet moments, he hoisted his body out of the co-pilot seat to go change clothes as requested, patting Antony on the shoulder to reassure the pilot, and himself, all would be fine. Everett didn't want to skydive into the night, but neither did he want his concerned employee to worry. "I trust you, Antony. And when we get to D.C., I'll buy the beer and we'll laugh about this together."

Everett pulled the curtain behind him as he continued to the cabin. He was usually the one giving orders, but he followed Antony's instructions with swift, efficient motions rather than waste time pondering the bizarre turn of events. As Everett buckled the parachute straps, he half-expected Antony to call back, laughing, and tell him this was a joke and *boy, you shoulda seen your face, Boss.* Except Antony didn't joke.

What the fuck was going on that had Antony suspicious and Everett waiting for the signal to jump out of a perfectly good airplane? Could all those bizarre events—all that *wacky shit*—be mere coincidence? Yes. But he'd never doubted the wisdom of Antony's gut feelings before, even as he insisted on making his own decisions based solely on fact and numbers. When Everett got back to the office from his meeting with the DCO, solving this mystery would be priority one.

The plane banked sharply to the side and dipped earthward, taking Everett's stomach on a roiling ride as he careened into a side console. The low-pressure light blinked, its flashing illumination a blaring klaxon horn in his head.

"Antony, what's going on?" Everett yelled over the pounding of his heart in his ears. "What's wrong?"

No answer, although Antony had surely heard him call out. The curtain parted and swayed from the aggressive angles of flight, giving Everett a view of the cockpit. His pilot now clenched the yoke with both hands, knuckles white and muscles strained. Antony turned his head toward Everett, his cyborg eyes glowing red like a demon's and his stoic face hard, emotionless lines of intent. The change was both subtle and shocking. However it had happened, his once reserved and competent pilot was gone, leaving in his place a creature intent on destruction.

With a push on the yoke, the plane's angle of descent sharpened and Everett stumbled toward the door. Antony's voice, strained and harsh, reached his ears. "B-boss… s-sorry."

His gut in his throat, Everett grabbed the door handle and took a deep breath from the oxygen tank. "Me, too, Antony."

He sent a prayer for his pilot, hefted the door open, and jumped clear.

Chapter Three

"Charlie! I haven't seen you in forever." Betty glanced up from her computer and smiled at the vagrant who'd entered the library. The four days since her altercation with Paul the Asshole had been quiet on a mind-numbing scale, and a visitor was a welcome sight. An irregular but friendly and respectful patron, Charlie looked like he always did. Scruffy beard and overgrown hair paired with worn clothing a size or two larger than necessary, hiding his slender build made even more slender from deprivation. All of it in a similar shade of unwashed brown, which wasn't unusual given his living situation.

Although her homeless days were *cough!*cough!* years ago, the memory of them were imprinted in her DNA. A special kind of hunger had been her constant companion those days. More than the pointed lack of possessions or clean clothes or roof over her head. More than physical starvation for food. More than the gaping maw of emptiness that had forced her to barter her body in exchange for meager provisions which still weren't enough to sustain the resulting child she'd tried, and failed, to carry in her womb. Although her body had breathed air and pumped blood, she might as well have been dead for all society cared. Civilization had refused to see her. Did not want to acknowledge her existence because doing so made its collective whole... uncomfortable... with its own moral compass. Society chose to ignore those who lived on the tenuous edge because it was easier to look away and walk around a problem than it was to walk hand-in-hand with it or try to solve it.

Ironic was the fact she had once thought becoming a cyborg might change that. She thought she would help her country as a 007 sort of spy. In reality, she had been nothing more than a high-end escort for aging government officials. She hadn't engaged in activities any more unpleasant as a so-called cyborg spy than she had while living on the streets. Aside from access to a better wardrobe and bed partners which skewed older, whiter, and richer, there was barely any difference between the two. Which was the true crime, because being a cyborg was supposed to have improved her lifestyle, not maintain it.

"Morning, Miss B. How've you been?" Charlie glanced around, tilting his head to peek down the rows of bookshelves.

"No need to be skittish, hon. We're alone." Betty walked around to his side of the desk and leaned a hip against it. "Listen, I packed too much food for lunch and I'd hate to see it go to waste. Care to join me?"

She made a habit of packing extra food. Others might ignore the souls camped in dark corners and doorways, but not Betty. The additional sandwiches and pieces of fruit were a meager, but welcome, offering for many. Oddly enough, Charlie rarely accepted her invitation.

He tucked his hands in the deep pockets of his baggy pants and stared at the floor, his body folding in on itself. An unconscious instinct to reflect society's disregard. "You're a good one, Miss B. But no, I just came to pass along an invitation."

"If you're trying to sell me oceanfront property in the hills of

Brown County, I'll have to politely decline." She teased him. He was far too young to be this serious.

"Dang, ya got me there." Charlie shook his head at the joke, but didn't laugh. He lifted his gaze to hers. "You 'member a gal who came in here a week or so ago? Tall. Skinny. 'Bout your age. Reddish brown hair."

Betty laughed. "The woman with the legs that could span the Indy 500 track? She told me I should be a model so I directed her to the fantasy section. What about her?"

What about her, aside from the fact she had used the library's computers to email the crackerjack reporter Candice Abara, who'd built a career on investigative stories about corruption in the cybernetics industry, and who'd then become suspiciously silent on the topic. The woman with the long legs had raced from the library shortly after, and hadn't even bothered to delete her cookies, much less close her internet tabs. Betty had walked back to find the computer monitor scrolling news about the death of Preditech's missing financial exec, Eve Myer. If the picture on the online obituary posting was accurate, the woman with the legs was Eve. Well, *had been* Eve. Eve Myer was considered dead to the world.

So why was Charlie talking about a supposedly dead woman?

"Yeah, *legs* is about right." He grunted, the sound as close to a laugh as Betty had ever heard from the young man. "She asked me to pass along that she'd like to meet with you. Says you two might have common interests."

Ice formed in Betty's gut. Why would a former Preditech exec want to meet with her? "Meet? What, like as in a date? A Girls Night Out? Are we going to drink wine and whine about men?"

She couldn't hide the defensive tone in her voice or stop the clench of her jaw. Over the last few years, no one had asked to meet with her. That was the point of living a lay-low sort of lifestyle. While in the service, most of her so-called *meetings* had been along the lines of seduction and infiltration. Actually, they hadn't been *meetings* at all. Spies don't have *meetings,* they have *targets.* And escorts don't have *targets,* they have *tricks.* And she hadn't had any of that; she'd had *clients,* as her handler had called them.

And cyborgs merely have brief interactions which they hope don't reveal their cybernetic status. Otherwise, the knowledge might incite a public panic and they might get burned at the stake. Pitchforks and torches would not be unexpected, a sad fact which clawed at Betty's tenuous faith in humanity.

Why would someone seek her out now, several years after she'd run away from her consignment as a spy? More importantly, why would a person who wasn't even supposed to be alive seek her out? No legitimate reason came to mind, so she fell back on the residual worry it might expose her cyborg status, whether purposefully or inadvertently. There was no way she would risk it. Before she'd run away from D.C., she had dug out the modem chip implanted in the back of her neck so her handler couldn't track or contact her. And he hadn't in all the years since. But paranoia remained a constant companion.

"Not my place to speculate why she wants to meet with you, Miss B." Charlie shrugged.

"And why did she ask *you* to come extend this invitation?" What was Charlie's relationship with Eve Myer that she trusted him with this task?

"I was gonna be in the area." Charlie shrugged again, staring at a shadow passing outside the front window. He faced her. "For what it's worth, I think you two would get along."

"And you know either of us well enough to make such a statement?" Her eyebrows lifted, much like her mother so many years ago when catching Betty in a lie. This was an expression she had seen on her mother many times. Betty had gotten much better at duplicity since then, a skill she took no pride in.

Charlie shrugged and shuffled toward the door. "I don't. But you both offer me food when no one else does. That's gotta mean something."

She opened her mouth to explain how that was hardly a reliable means of character assessment, but the door opened with an rush of air, barring Charlie from her line of sight and drawing her attention to the unfamiliar vagrant who stepped into the library. Greasy hair that was likely blond and some scraggly growth of facial hair that was barely a beard, but he had all the bone structure of a handsome man, including height and broad shoulders which hadn't yet caved and drooped from the weight of society's indifference. As filthy as they were, his clothes still smelled of money, even with all the wrinkles, rips, and stains. If Armani had a homeless chic line, he could be their runway model.

But not all displaced people were ugly, and not all cast-off clothes were rags. Betty reached out her hand. "Welcome to the Greater Broad Ripple Public Library, hon. I'm Betty."

His handshake was firm with confidence. "Hello, Betty. I'm, Ev—um, I'm… Clark."

The gravelly tone of his voice pebbled across her skin and the warmth of his hand engulfing hers zinged along her spine. These were bygone sensations, distant memories of more naïve times when she indulged in sexual attraction. But no longer. Not if she wanted to remain safe. So she pulled her hand from his and twined her fingers against her belly. "Can I help you find something to read, Clark? Political Thriller? Suspense? Biographies? Sports—"

"Uh, well, I'd like to use a computer, if you have one."

Betty swallowed her disappointment. Seemed like no one read for pleasure these days. Sure, she might entice Charlie with a graphic novel on occasion, but his visits were rare and—wait, where was he? She glanced around the room, but there was no sight of him. Had he snuck out while she'd welcomed Clark?

Probably. The man had ninja stealth skills. If he wasn't so young, she might suspect he'd been recruited by the government like she had.

The theory might explain why he'd approached her about meeting with Eve. All the more reason for Betty to have declined.

Clark cleared his throat, bringing her attention back to him. "So do you? Have a computer I could use?"

Standing inside, without the light of day shining from behind, his features were more visible. Like the pewter color of his eyes, surrounded by dark spiky lashes and straight, no-nonsense eyebrows. The crinkles around his eyes and the lines written across his forehead indicated he was around her age. As did the white patches of facial hair around his chin and the silver at the temple of his slight receding hairline. Together, it lent him the stately, dignified appearance of a self-assured middle-aged man.

And wasn't that a bitch-slap from life. Betty spent hours meticulously grooming and artfully applying makeup to minimize time's effect, and here a homeless man who'd probably never been within a yard of tweezers beat her at aging gracefully.

"Yes, we have computers you may use. Let me show you the way." She didn't sound irritated, did she? Or resentful? He wasn't at fault for being born with good genes while hers had come from the thrift store sale rack along with her luck.

Pasting on a pleasant smile, she led the way toward the back of the library to the short row of computers. She could have simply pointed the way, since he couldn't get lost in the tiny library. But customer service was one of her priorities. She insisted on going the extra mile to welcome all guests, a policy which included personally escorting Clark to the area to point out the Li-Fi password and answer any questions he might—

Ugh. She was jerking her own chain. Call her bored, call her a snoop, but investigating the sites people visited while tucked away in the back of the library entertained her. Clark's first impression had piqued her interest, so she wanted to know more about him. Like what sites he would visit. And why he walked and talked like a successful business executive but looked like the world had kicked him to the curb.

Yeah, she was definitely bored.

"Here they are." She waved toward the three computers at a back table near the reference kiosks. "A generous patron donated these a few years ago. They were outdated even then, but should still work for your needs unless you want to stream movies or battle with your gamer buddies."

Clark stared at the computers and nodded, but she got the impression he only half-listened to her. His hands hung casually from the front pockets of his dress khakis, ripped at the knees and smudged with grass and mud. His button-down shirt, as rumpled as it was and stained at the pits, fit him better than it should. Better than anything off the rack would fit anyone. Fit him like it had been tailored for his lean runner's physique. And, although his loafers were scuffed and dirty, they hadn't seen many miles. He scratched the whiskers along his jaw as more of a reflex than a conscious motion, and the move niggled in the back of her head. Some sort of déjà vu or memory. But she'd never seen Clark before. The library saw few enough patrons, she remembered nearly all of them from over the years, and he wasn't one. Still, something about him seemed familiar.

Betty cleared her throat to get the both of them out of their own thoughts and back into the moment. "Is there anything I can help you search? Offer helpful websites for whatever you're looking for?"

He frowned and shook his head, his gaze flicking in her direction before darting back to the computers. "No. No thank you, Betty. I think I can find what I need. But I appreciate the offer."

"Okay. I'll leave you to it. Yell if you need something. We close at five."

With the barest nod in her direction, he pulled up to a computer, setting his cross-body satchel on the chair next to him then tugging it closer, obviously not trusting the few possessions he had were safe anywhere but within immediate reach. The sentiment was common and understandable. The homeless had so little to call their own, and had to carry it all with them or risk losing it. But his possessions happened to be in a three-hundred dollar designer shoulder pack that looked brand new.

Betty walked back to the front desk, pondering the enigma seated at the computers. He might be down on his luck, but whoever Clark was, he wasn't homeless.

Chapter Four

E verett had never been this repulsive in all his life. Not even years ago when he'd cloistered himself for months in his rundown apartment-slash-makeshift-laboratory, living on ramen noodles and energy drinks like some mad scientist while he developed his breakthrough cybernetic system. His time in a slumlord's neglected efficiency had nothing on the last four days he'd spent in the same underwear, hiking past acres of Indiana corn and soybean fields in the August heat, fermenting a crotch kombucha in his pants. Not to mention the layer of fuzz he'd grown in his mouth or the chemistry experiment of sunscreen and bug repellent layered on his face. And he refused to think about the acidic stench of his armpits.

Not the impression he was accustomed to giving, especially to women as beautiful as Betty the librarian. His male pride winced. Women usually fell at his feet because he was rich and connected, not from the noxious fumes of his body odor. But Betty had been kind enough not to gag in disgust, which placed her in a class above the socialites of his Chicago circles. Those vipers would turn away from him in his current state. They'd also scoff at Betty's old school pinup model look, but there was no denying the sex appeal of her retro style and forthright manner. Her gracious welcome, calm and confident. Her bowtie lips painted an enticing combination of innocent pout and come-fuck-me fullness. Her womanly curves promised both thrills and comfort.

Damn it, she was absolutely his type. But there was no way she'd be into him in his current state, not that she'd necessarily be into him if he had access to clean clothes and a shower. Betty hadn't recoiled from him, but that didn't mean she'd welcome his advances or even a subtle flirtation. In her eyes, he was no doubt merely a—

Dickhead! Everett bit the inside of his cheek. Here he was whining about personal hygiene and thinking about the lovely librarian, when someone out there wanted him dead and Antony had made the ultimate sacrifice for it. He'd warned Everett and prepared him and saved his ignorant ass, then died for him. Everett was an ungrateful fuckwit for forgetting that fact.

As he had parachuted down to the middle of farm country in the late-night darkness, he'd watched his jet and pilot nosedive into the ground and the resulting fiery explosion. Plummeting at full throttle with a full tank of fuel straight into the flat landscape of northern Indiana, the flames had probably been visible in the next county. The wail of fire trucks and police cars, the flashing lights of emergency vehicles racing past, had pierced the peaceful rural night.

For the past four days, Everett had nothing to do but think and walk. Think and walk past miles of farm fields. Think and walk around one-stoplight towns. Think and walk and pine for his self-drive car and hope the few people who passed him didn't recognize him. If Antony had been right and someone was trying to kill Everett, being recognized could be detrimental to staying alive.

The closer he'd gotten to the state capital Indianapolis—the closer to a metropolitan city teeming with masses of humanity—

the more his situation seemed like a fever dream. While he trudged mile after mile away from the crash scene, authorities were no doubt sifting through ashes and shrapnel to learn the truth of why the plane had gone down, probably assuming pilot error. Would they find evidence of Antony's cybernetic brain being hacked? Would they even find enough of Antony's cybernetic brain to piece it together? And did Everett want them to? Society mistrusted cyborgs enough as it was. If word got out that cyborgs could be hacked and forced to do something against their will, it would dogpile on the fake news spread by his computer virus. Preditech would be crushed under more bad PR, and its bottom line shattered.

The only saving grace—if it could be called that—was the morbid fact authorities would find only fragments of charred bones they'd have to DNA match to confirm the death of both pilot and passenger. The process could take months to years, if they were interested at all in finding the truth. Everett had time to get to the bottom of this fucked-up mystery, hopefully before whoever wanted him dead realized he wasn't. Hopefully before word got out hackers could use cyborgs as highly destructive weapons. And most hopefully before his company sustained any irreparable damage.

Antony had talked like he might be forced to do something against his wishes. Like he was nothing more than a mindless computer. But who could do such a thing to a cyborg? All Preditech's cybernetic systems were encrypted so only the software manufacturer could access them for download updates. But the software manufacturer was another company, another branch of the DCO. What if—?

What if what? Everett still had no idea what, if anything, was going on. The combination of Antony's words, the jet crash, the network virus, and Eve Myer's weird disappearance…when considered individually were merely odd occurrences, but lumped together were *some wacky shit*. Damn, he was as paranoid as Antony. So much for following logic. Logic couldn't ignore the possible connection of these events, and that left a vague stirring of unease in his gut.

Everett's stomach growled. "Or maybe I'm just hungry," he muttered, huffing a bitter laugh at his own rampant thoughts.

"Listen Clark, I packed too much food for lunch today. Would you like some?"

Betty's angelic voice pulled his attention back to the present. She stood at the other end of the short table, a living contradiction with her classic pinup style. Her hourglass figure and bold lips screamed sin, but her pastel pink, flared-skirt gingham dress with its button-up collar and hint of white cotton petticoat beneath was all innocence. Then again, a woman who had reached her age would naturally be a little of both, and so much more. Her vibrant red hair in soft curls cascaded to her shoulders, tucked away from her face with a sweet spray of pink roses. The seductive upward sweep of her eyeliner. The prim wrist-length white gloves. The high-heeled wedge mules with hot pink flames across the bridge.

Everett's mouth watered, and not just from the offer of food.

Her face scrunched with confusion. "Do you need help turning to computer on?"

He glanced at the blank screen staring back at him and scrubbed his face with a hand. "I, uh, kinda zoned out. Sorry."

Betty sat a hip on the edge of the table. Even wearing her heels, the height forced her supporting leg straight to her tiptoes, and her skirt hitched, exposing a dimpled knee. The pose was as deceptively sexy as any of those he'd seen from the women of Chicago's upper crust. Those she-sharks did nothing without careful consideration as to the precise impact on unsuspecting bits of husband chum. He'd nearly been caught in those jaws before. Never again.

Even so, he could still appreciate the view.

Betty nestled her hands in her lap and leaned toward him. "Clark, where have you been sleeping?"

Okay, not a conversation topic he was used to. But, this wasn't a meeting with his execs or a society party. If he was going to assume everyone was out to get him, he needed to guard personal details. Especially those personal details which could be easily traced. Fortunately, he'd had the presence of mind not to blurt his actual name earlier. The name his maternal grandmother would have been given had she been a boy wasn't in any data records anywhere. The fact he was the only living person privy to that bit of family folklore was convenient.

Betty waited patiently for his answer, the soft glow of sympathy around her head like a halo. She might be beautiful, but she was just the kind of nosy do-gooder who would slather him in self-righteous pity and make him her personal lost cause until she could get him back on his feet and a functioning member of society.

And he couldn't tell her he already was. Or at least, that he had been until a few nights ago.

He leaned back and crossed his legs at the ankle. "Well, Betty. I had reservations at the Ritz, but they wouldn't give me double points on my rewards account, so I canceled."

She stared at him for a few seconds before leaning one hand on the table and the other on her hip, a half-smirk on her lips. "Can't say I blame you. You get much better turn-down service at the park, but only if you score a bench. I've also heard that down by the river is comfy, if you don't mind a lower thread count."

"But will they validate my parking?"

She studied her fingernails. "I don't really know. I always use a car service, and my driver takes care of such minutia."

Oddly enough, she played along with his bullshit. She even managed an air of jaded ennui. Everett couldn't help the rough chuckle that crawled up his throat. Betty tilted her head and smiled, and damn if the expression didn't look every bit like *don't be an ass.* Miss Librarian wasn't a pushover even if her clothing choices were from a more deferential era.

His stomach seized that moment to growl again like a cornered beast, wiping away any protest he might have made for accepting her offer of food. The softening of her smile contradicted the flash of triumph in her moss-green eyes. "You're obviously hungry. But I also understand you might have your reasons for not taking me up on my offer, and I won't force or harass you. It's your choice."

Uh, were they still talking food? Why did she make such a big deal about his decision to eat her lunch? Truth was, he was hungry. He'd lived four days with only the couple of apples and granola bars Antony had packed in his suspicious foresight. It wasn't enough to sustain Everett for long, but enough to stave off making the leap into stealing food or dumpster diving.

"I can't repay you for the food." Damn, it rankled to have to accept a handout. Nothing was free in his world. And acts of kindness always came with strings attached.

"If I had expected you to pay, I would have led with that detail." Betty stood. "How about this: I'm real messy in the kitchen. I'm going to go make my own lunch, and if stuff happens to fall onto another plate in the process, I'll let you have it. Fair?"

Everett nodded at her back as she walked away. Trying to match wits with her wasn't getting him the answers he needed. He swiveled around to the computer and turned it on. The antique lumbered to the home screen with all the speed of watching paint dry. If this were his office, he'd have replaced it before it could process its first startup command. However, this ancient model was a blessing because it didn't have all the keystroke tracking features new models did. He could conduct his online searches with almost complete anonymity. A blessing indeed, considering where his searches might lead him. If he was careless, he'd be tracked to this library.

Hopefully his teen hacker skills weren't too outdated. He pulled up the *Chicago Tribune* online and tweaked its ad- and graphic-heavy stream so it wouldn't impede his secondary search. Even a stationary pop-up ad like what only the most outdated companies still used could be the death of this dinosaur computer. He dug in, drilling down into the dark web and gray web and system backdoors. The scenery might have changed over the decades, but the paths were still familiar. The passcodes had gotten more complex, but he enjoyed the challenge. Who would have thought the thrill of pushing the cybernetic envelope would pale in comparison to his current foray into the underbelly of the internet?

Once a delinquent, always a delinquent.

His fingers paused on the keyboards, enthusiasm for the task at hand deflated. He could drape himself in pricey designer labels and slap a fancy job title on his office door. But at his core, he was still a kid unburdened by the attention and oversight of caring parents, overstepping the line of propriety and walking the path no one else had noticed. Because he could, and because no one was there to tell him not to. That habit had gotten him sent to jail as a minor. It has also helped him achieve his greatest success as an adult. And a few days ago, it had nearly gotten him killed.

And might still.

Once he reached Preditech's network, he faced the real challenge. He had designed it himself to be impenetrable. Fortunately, he knew what to look for, and could disable the alarms Eve—or someone pretending to be Eve—had tripped when she'd checked her company email. He also counted on the hope no one had ramped up surveillance of the system in the wake of his supposed death.

How fucked up was his world that it was a good thing everyone assumed he was dead?

The soft clap of Betty's heels against the soles of her feet sounded as she approached, pulling his thoughts back to the present. With a quick keyboard command, the *Tribune* page flicked to the front and he turned to smile as she set a plate on the table near the computer. He nearly choked. Dear God, how much lunch had she packed? This was a feast. A thick sandwich on artisanal bread, a pile of homemade chips, and a square of chocolatey deliciousness the size of his hand.

"You weren't lying about being messy." Well, that came out a tad ungrateful. He coughed and tried to recover. "Thank you. I hope some food actually made it to your plate."

"Don't worry, I have plenty to eat." Betty chuckled as she set a glass of water next to the plate. "I didn't know what you like to drink."

If she'd placed a glass of twenty-five-year-old single-malt scotch in front of him, he wouldn't have been half this thrilled. One, because he was more of a gin man. And two, because he hadn't had a drink that didn't come from a dirty puddle or pond since his glass of wine at dinner four nights ago. His hands trembled as he lifted the glass of clear liquid to his lips.

"It might taste funny. It's just tap water." She cautioned.

Everett drank the entire contents of the glass before setting it back down with a satisfied sigh. "It tastes cold and wet, exactly how I like it."

"Obviously." Betty smiled, a thread of humor in her voice. She nodded toward the computer screen. "The library has a subscription to The Indianapolis Star if you prefer local news."

Shit, that would have made more sense as a facade. He scratched his jawline. How could he explain this choice without divulging any personal information? "Old habit. It's what my dad read when I was little, and I just... continued the tradition, I guess."

Personal information like that. Everett glanced away from Betty and her too-perceptive stare. *Stupid.* Why had he told her the truth? That little tidbit wasn't enough for anyone to find out who he was or why he was here, but he couldn't get in the habit of blurting truth. Not now.

A warm hand squeezed his shoulder, bringing his attention back to her lovely face. "I understand, Clark." Betty's voice was soft. And a little sad. "Sometimes it's the little things that keep us connected to our past. And those days take on a more halcyon level of comfort the further in our rearview they are, don't they." Her smile dimmed for the briefest moment before she rallied and plucked up his glass. "I'll bring you more water, then I'll leave you to your lunch and research."

She walked away, the sway of her hips enthralling. Betty was naturally sexy, like the women in his social circles. The difference was, those predators wouldn't have given him a second glance if they saw him in his current condition. They had no time for dirty and destitute. They would not have shared their lunch or offered any words of comfort, and certainly not words that sounded like they came from a deep well of personal experience.

So why had Betty?

Chapter Five

Betty uploaded her latest book review to the library website, then opened the events calendar to update. Tomorrow's monthly Toddler Time story program always drew a small crowd of mothers looking for a change-up in their daily routine, and she relished the chance to instill the joy of reading in young children. Plus, she got to interact with actual people. The thought trembled in her bones like a kid on Christmas morning.

Or maybe that thread of anticipation had more to do with the man sitting at the library computers. She shook her head against the thought, as if doing so negated its possibility.

She jotted down an outline of tasks and activity supplies to prepare for tomorrow's event. Then underlined the tasks. Starred the supplies. Drew flowers by the crucial ones. Dotted the page with butterflies, small hearts, angry skulls, lightning bolts, and daggers. Anything to keep her backside in her chair and away from Clark. Anything to resist the tug of intrigue he presented.

A tiny bug of curiosity buzzed around the inside of her head, demanding she approach him again and make conversation. But she'd already interrupted him three times since bringing him lunch. At this point, another interruption for anything short of a natural disaster would be ridiculous. In the span of a couple hours, she'd effectively transitioned from *bored*, straight past *snoop*, and into full-on *stalker*.

What was he doing back there? What was he searching for? Why had he looked so shocked when he'd shared the bit about his father? What had brought him to his current state?

Everyone had their individual story, even the displaced, and Betty never probed. To badger someone into explaining why they lived in a cardboard box down by the river was as rude as expecting a person to share the details of their finances or sex life. Yes, she was a snoop, but some things should be shared willingly and only when the sharer felt safe in doing so.

Still, she practically vibrated with the desire to know more about Clark.

He didn't... *act* homeless. Or even down on his luck. He carried himself with all the confidence and authority of a successful businessman. His jokes about the Ritz lacked the bitterness she expected from someone suffering the wrongs of the world. And his shoulder beneath her hand had been sturdy and muscular, not tired and undernourished. He acted less destitute and more... someone acting the part of being destitute.

Heavens, it made no sense, even in her own brain. But there it was, a little bug buzzing and bouncing around her head, trying to land on what, exactly, Clark was. What about him triggered her interest with such intensity. A tenuous, evasive answer, for sure, and unrelated to her unsated lust even as he piqued her womanly interest. But it was something more. He seemed familiar. She recognized something about him, beyond the designer labels he wore.

And that terrified her.

She chewed back the panic rising in her chest. His looks, his manner, his voice... *Something*... Something about Clark reminded her of... someone she'd known. Like the reflection of a ghost, his behavior echoed with familiarity in her bones. Her gut was certain she'd known him. Unfortunately, her gut wasn't equipped to answer the question *how.*

Only her cybernetic parts could solve that mystery.

Nibbling her bottom lip, she braced her resolve with a deep inhalation and started up the CPU part of her brain. It flickered on instantly like a fresh bulb. No, wrong image. The damn thing never turned off, she simply avoided actively using it. Using its advanced capabilities and the data stored there seemed an unfair advantage for one human to have over others. It reminded her of just how different her cybernetic systems made her from everyone else. Little wonder the public was terrified of cyborgs. She was a little frightened of herself.

But apparently not so scared she refused to use it where Clark was concerned. She scanned databases of important people, news articles she'd uploaded over the years, even psychological documentation to determine which of his behaviors could be classified as deception. Unfortunately, when she'd torn out her modem, her automatic CPU updates had ceased. The data was several years old and intermingled with the thousands of romance plotlines and characters she'd read since then. Filtering through what was fact and what was fiction made her head throb.

"No, Clark was the name of the main character in the brothers-best-friend story that was so popular last year." She muttered as she rubbed her temples. "Grey was the name of that one billionaire guy... not the color of his eyes. And the cyborg espionage whistle blower was a sci-fi romance story from a few decades ago."

I think. Truth was, she couldn't be certain of anything. If she wanted to truly figure out why thoughts of Clark tripped her memories, she needed to talk to him. Keeping her distance, even though it was the courteous thing to do for a patron, would not help answer her questions about him. It would only dredge up more.

But she needed a plausible excuse, else she risked scaring him away. She opened a bottom drawer in her desk and pulled out one of the amenities bags she kept on hand in case of emergencies. A small bar of soap, washrag, toothbrush, and toothpaste were all she could offer to a homeless person such as Clark. It wasn't much, but maybe it would be enough.

As she approached the computer area, his growling voice reached her ears. "Ratfink motherfucker" followed the slam of a fist on the table. Rather than sneak up on him, she gripped her toes so her shoes batted loudly against the bottoms of her feet with each step. Like the several other times she'd approached before, he switched tabs as she came within eyesight, bringing forth the *Trib's* front page, and turned to her expectantly.

Or was that his guilty expression?

He looked every bit the child caught in the cookie jar. It didn't require running her body language interpreting program to know he was snooping around parts of the internet he shouldn't be. The real questions were which sites, how dangerous was his search, and how at risk was the library for getting caught in someone's crosshairs?

"Here to offer me another delicious brownie?"

He flashed her a hopeful smile as she settled a hip against the table. Or was that question a diversion tactic? Instead of answering either of their questions, she dangled the amenities baggie and smiled. "I'm sorry to bother you yet again, Clark. But I found this in my drawer and thought you could use it."

He reached out and palmed the bag, looking at its contents as if she'd offered him priceless jewels. Given his current situation, her offering was likely just as precious. He looked up. "Don't suppose the library has a shower?"

His expression was stripped of all guise. *This* was what hope looked like on Clark, which answered her unspoken question: his previous expression had been pretend. She shook her head. "Unfortunately, we only have a single-toilet bathroom with a sink and a hand dryer. But it locks. And you're the only patron here, so feel free to take your time."

He glanced at the bag, then back at the computer as if hesitant to leave it. Or leave her with it. She stood as if to return to her desk, and patted him on the shoulder. The touch was unnecessary, but she liked the feel of his solid form beneath her fingers. Rather than make any false assurances, she simply smiled and left him to do as he wished. She couldn't push too hard or he might turn tail and run. Coaxing a wild animal required small, gentle advances to build trust. The same with any vagrant who'd experienced the harshness humanity could offer.

He stayed at the computer for a few more minutes. Likely backtracking out of wherever he'd been. Possibly even scrubbing his footprints so no one could trace them. Betty bit back a chuckle. If Clark was savvy enough, that tactic might work on a cyber-investigator. But not her. She was part computer herself, fluent in the language of those little zeros and ones and equipped with a fingertip datajack for easy access to whatever computer she wanted thanks to her cyborg spy upgrades. These days, this particular skill was rarely used, even when she wanted to know what patrons did while on the library computers. Anyone with a half-hearted IT education could track those digital footprints. And ninety-five percent of the time, they led to either job recruitment sites or porn.

Surely Clark wasn't watching porn. Maybe she shouldn't have blindly offered him a washrag and invited him to lock himself in the bathroom.

The click of him doing just that echoed softly in the silence of the library. Her legs flinched instinctively, her body screaming to run to the computers and download as much information as she could before he finished. She gripped the edge of her desk to halt the reaction. "This is your library. You have the keys. The computers are not going anywhere." She whispered the mantra to the ceiling. This was not one of her spy assignments, time working against her to accomplish whatever task she'd been given. She did not have to seduce the target—

Dark memories flickered in the back of her head like an ancient movie camera groaning to life only to die again. Unrecognizable. Elusive. Disjointed. Strangers, yet mildly familiar, danced in her head. Men. Women. Targets, all of them, she was certain. She felt that truth in her bones. But who they were remained a question her CPU could not—would not—answer.

These were memories buried so deep in her cortex as to be ghosts. Possibly apparitions of her imagination. Recollections of the three years she spent as a cybernetic spy-slash-escort were spotty at best. She recalled government parties spent flirting with the evening's target, surrounded by the aromas of self-importance and imported caviar. Private gatherings draped on the arms of powerful men. Clandestine meetings in hotel rooms and empty boardrooms with some pompous elected official. She couldn't picture faces, but couldn't forget how those aging men —and occasionally women—looked at her like she was property. Remembered their smells and flavors, the way their touches oozed along her skin and scraped at her nerves. These sordid snippets blended into one overwhelming sensation of empty dust and sour ruin, as if their souls were rotten and seeping into the essence of their bodies.

Or maybe it was Betty's tattered soul leeching into her own flesh.

She had no memory of sex with any of her targets, only a general sense of regret and self-loathing when she awoke alone and in her own bed the following day, chunks of time lost and unaccounted for. She couldn't remember names, the sex which surely followed, or the intel she assumed she'd been ordered to gather with her datajack finger. But any sane person would connect the dots and believe the missing times were merely a continuation of the trajectory where the memory left off. It explained why her *clients* had looked at her as if they were already buried deep inside her.

Perhaps she'd subconsciously blocked those memories, like trauma victims or soldiers suffering PTSD. Perhaps those memories had been deleted from her CPU. If what she remembered was this unpalatable, how disgusting must the missing parts be? How sordid the sex with these men and women? And did she really want to know?

Those memories were no doubt sullied, like her. She might wear the trappings of old-timey decency, but she was damaged goods. Had been before she'd become a cyborg, and was now even more so.

So the mere thought of digging deep enough to unlock her Pandora's Box of memories shot bile up her throat and ice to her nerves. Her body shook with the need to avoid unearthing those particular forgotten details. To run away, as if she could put physical distance between her body and her forgotten memories. She jackknifed to her feet and swept a trembling hand down the few wrinkles along the front of her skirt to calm herself.

As she finished, the bell above the door chimed.

Pasting on her welcome smile, she looked up to greet her new patron. Her smile faltered. Talk about bad memories. The asshole Paul from a few days ago stood in the entryway, a bandage across the bridge of his nose where she'd whacked him with the door and twin half-moon bruises under his eyes. Two men who appeared equally as gruff and unpleasant flanked him. Betty carefully placed her hands atop the desk in an attempt to calm her jitters and appear non-aggressive. Tension rolled off the three men as potently as did the smell of cheap alcohol, mixing with her own taut emotions.

Paul chuckled and sauntered into the library like a king. No, wrong imagery. Like a pirate who assumed he'd earned the right to the treasure before him. He staggered a step, his inebriated state a chink in the armor of his cockiness. He jerked his chin at her and ran his tongue along his teeth with a loud sucking sound. Was that supposed to terrify her? Arouse her? It only served to churn her stomach further.

"Good afternoon, gentlemen. Welcome to the Greater Broad Ripple Public Library. Can I recommend a book for you?"

A lopsided smirk, likely meant to be rakish or inviting, added a goofy nuance to Paul's drunken state. "Nah. I'm looking at whut I want."

She played dumb, glancing behind her to the holographic periodicals kiosk against the wall before gifting him with her most angelic smile. "Excellent choice. Those are the newest 'zines to celebrate the upcoming National Transgender Awareness Week."

A lie. That week wasn't until November and the holo-zines currently on display were the rote fashion ones. But Paul didn't know. His jaw dropped and he squinted at the wall, swaying from the effort. She almost pitied him, trying to match wits when he could barely stand.

He growled. "I'm not talking 'bout those fag rags."

Fag rags? Any remorse she might have harbored evaporated with his comment. He was checking off all the Total Asshole boxes, and she steeled for battle.

He continued, his words slurring. "I'm talking 'bout you. I wuz here a few days ago. Got you so hot 'n bothered you couldn't walk straight." He nudged one of his thug pals like they were in on a private joke, and the three men chortled. Paul speared her with another glare, his face transforming into a mask of loathing. As if she was still the cause for his woes.

Because she had soooo much influence in his life and nothing else to do with hers but make him miserable. Her eyeballs hurt from the effort not to roll.

Betty nodded her chin to indicate Paul's face. "You're the one with a broken nose. A better indication *you* couldn't walk straight." She eased around to the front of her desk and leaned her backside against it. A better defensive position than already backed into a corner, should they attack. "You know, Neanderthal romance isn't a genre, but we have plenty of medieval historicals and even a selection of non-con over in row three you might find interesting."

While his buddies seemed confused by her words, Paul didn't take the bait this time. Or perhaps he was too drunk to multi-task hearing and processing. He continued to leer at her. "I didn't finish whut we started, so invited my frenz to have a lil' fun, too. I'd say lay back 'n enjoy the ride, but I'm kinda hopin' you put up a fight."

Aaaaand there was the last Total Asshole box. *Check.*

Chapter Six

Everett squeezed the excess warm water from the soapy cloth and scrubbed his armpits with all the vigor of a dental hygienist on tooth plaque. Speaking of which, he swiped his tongue across his minty-fresh teeth and vowed never again to take the sensation for granted.

Locked in the library restroom, he washed his face and hair in the sink, and then the rancid crevices of his body as best as he could, drying with the air-dryer and shaking his head at what an awkward picture he must make wearing nothing but socks and spreading his ass cheeks beneath the blowing nozzle. It wasn't a bath at The Carlyle, but washing off at least a few layers of sweat and grime was luxurious. Like he'd sloughed away the taint of lies and deceit with each pass of the washcloth, leaving him refreshed and renewed.

Only he wasn't. He still had to wear his filthy clothes. And he still had to keep his identity a secret and figure out why someone had planted a virus in his network and who had tried to kill him. Which meant the lies and deceit were still as present as before, except they now smelled of vanilla and lavender.

Betty didn't know any of this, and he couldn't tell her.

Couldn't *come clean* so to speak, even as a gesture of appreciation for her kindness. Even if he didn't need to keep his identity a secret, what could he possibly divulge that wouldn't make him sound unhinged? What he'd found during his search had been random at best, and a conspiracy theorist's wet dream at worst. And none of it had given him any warm fuzzies.

The internet was plastered with news about his death in a plane crash and speculations about the future of Preditech. As a privately-owned company, it didn't have a board of directors to make such crucial decisions. His own senior management staff could handle business as usual, but not the inferno of bad press the damn virus had ignited, and he wasn't there to defend his company. Of course, it all would be a moot issue now. As a result of his supposed death, his estate, including Preditech, would go through probate because he didn't have a will. Why would he? He hadn't planned on dying.

And that was the good news.

The bad news was, with the announced confirmation of his death—so much for thinking authorities might take the time to sift through the crash remains to verify—no will and no beneficiary to inherit his estate, and the lion's share of a cybernetic industry on the line, the government had swooped in and declared jurisdiction over both Preditech and the hundreds of patents Everett held. Admitting it was an unusual interpretation of eminent domain, the DCO claimed the company was simply too large and important to fail as a result of Everett's untimely passing. Official emails assured employees their livelihoods would continue without a hiccup, a public announcement would be made soon, and this is what Everett would have wanted for the company.

"Ratfink motherfu-grrrr!" Everett had growled at the discovery, moments before Betty had handed him the precious amenities bag. Fortunately, he'd heard her approach and it had distracted him from the need to scream and heave the entire computer table against the wall.

Even now, the urge to punch something clenched against his bones. His hands shook with impotent rage and he braced them on the edge of the bathroom sink. He'd never felt such powerful betrayal. Not when Hollywood had gotten rich on cyborg-snuff-style movies, thus painting him as a sort of Doctor Frankenstein and his life's work a monstrosity. Not when his high school frenemy had ratted him to the authorities and gotten him sent to juvie for hacking into his own father's bank account as a lark.

Not even when his iceberg of a father had declared Everett *no son of his and no longer his burden* over twenty stolen bucks and the disgrace of having been caught, and had left Everett in juvie to learn his lesson.

All his life's work would now become someone else's property with one broad sweep of government at its greediest. The remainder of his assets would go to distant family members once the state tracked them down. Or maybe they'd pop out of the woodwork at the thought of inheriting his wealth. Joke was on them. Other than his sparse apartment furniture, several pricey suits, and the scorched remnants of his crashed jet, there wasn't anything to inherit because Everett had reinvested everything into Preditech. His company was the glittering diamond of his fool's gold estate.

Most people didn't know this fact. But Richard Hawks, Director of the DCO did. He knew, and had clearly jumped at the chance to claim Preditech for his own.

"Thieving bastard." Everett growled through clenched teeth. "He can go fucking choke on his aviator sunglasses."

Hawks was an older version of Everett. Ambitious, driven, focused. A calculating predator with a take-no-prisoners attitude where his DCO responsibilities were concerned. Since the inception of the DCO and Hawks's assignment to head the Special Projects division, he and Everett had collaborated, tearing through technological obstacles and government red tape to forge a path for cybernetics. Everett had begun Preditech because it was an untapped market with a wealth of potential, specifically the potential to make him wealthy. The alpha phase of his systems had focused on helping first responders injured on the job, like Antony before he'd become a pilot. Police and Fire departments would happily pay for rehabilitation because it ultimately saved them money. And when they could also conveniently apply for government grants from the DCO to get their injured employees *enhanced,* well, why the hell not? Even as public opinion about cybernetic individuals had soured thanks to Hollywood and a few unhappy customers, the deal was a win-win situation for the local departments.

Everett, and therefore Preditech, had nursed that teat like starving calves. Hawks had requested specialized parts and programming, believing cyborgs could enhance national security. His vision had included using cybernetic systems for espionage and weaponry. Hawks had dangled funds in the amount of insanity. Money Everett could and did use to grow Preditech into the premier company it was today. Enough to turn Everett's black-and-white world into Technicolor; all he had to do was follow the yellow brick road. Hawks had bastardized the pursuit of cybernetic possibility, and Everett had followed him right down the golden path, turning a blind eye to the man pulling all the levers behind the curtain.

Everett had assumed Hawks could be trusted. Fellow apex predators like themselves were supposed to respect the boundaries of one another's territory, especially when hunting grounds were fertile with prey. But Hawks's current seizure of Preditech was an overt challenge. A bold invasion of Everett's arena. An assimilation of his Preditech pack into Hawks's own. And rather than fend off the raider, the Preditech senior staff welcomed him in like a conquering hero.

So much for the mutual respect men like Everett and Hawks

were supposed to offer one another. Hawks no doubt saw an opportunity and snatched it with all the militant precision and power available to him through the DCO. Hawks was opportunistic enough to yank Preditech under his wing at the first chance. Was he greedy enough to have premeditated that move?

Was he ruthless enough to have planned Everett's death?

Ice gripped his spine and nausea roiled his stomach. All the wacky shit that had been happening took on a new meaning. A far more personal and deadly meaning. More proof he was in deep shit and needed to get to the bottom of this rabbit hole before he ended up in his own hole, six-feet deep. Antony had claimed he had a *feeling*. Something in the pilot's gut had connected the random dots and believed they pointed at Everett. He was a target. Antony had told Everett to watch his back, but hadn't known who to suspect.

Everett knew. He'd connected the dots now and also had a *feeling*. A sinking in his gut because Hawks was no doubt behind it all, like a puppet master. The man Everett had thought could be trusted—the colleague he'd thought was eager to work *together* —had tossed him aside like so much useless trash.

Once again, Everett had been abandoned and forced to figure his own way out.

Using the angst still boiling in his veins, he wrenched the remaining drops of moisture out of the washrag and put the items back in the baggie. He was as clean as he could get, given the circumstances, although still soiled on a far more elemental level. Baggie in hand, he unlocked the bathroom door and headed to the front to thank Betty and offer up whatever menial payback he could.

As he approached the front, he heard another man's voice. Angry and slurred. Everett snuck down a row to observe without interfering. From his vantage point, he had a partial view of a bizarre standoff. Three burly, agitated men faced Betty, who rested with deceptive nonchalance against her desk. The clench of her jaw belied her casual stance, and a single eyebrow lifted in defiance. Everett's heart kicked into high gear. The tension rolling off all four a palpable entity. This was like watching a bomb about to detonate, and Everett was helpless to stop it.

"So? Are we gonna finish whut we started?" The man standing closest to Betty leered at her, his voice dripping with sexual intent. He was as tall and thick as the other two and looked like he ate nails for lunch. Everett's former daily work-out schedule hadn't included boxing or mixed martial arts, but he wasn't weak. Neither was he a match for three angry drunks. And Betty didn't even know he waited from a flanking position to come to her aid. She faced these three bruisers alone. Everett waited for her to defuse the situation. To paste on her warm librarian smile and say something to sooth them.

She didn't.

"Listen Paul, not being able to finish sounds like a medical condition you should discuss with your doctor, not a librarian." Betty's eyebrows knotted together as if in pained sympathy for the man's sexual dysfunction. The tone of her voice was clear she mocked him. She circled a finger at the two flunkies flanking the Paul guy. "And are these your only friends? Or are they the only ones drunk enough to help you rape me?"

Brute One and Brute Two glanced at each other. Had her words sobered them a bit? Had they not known Paul's intent when they'd agreed to follow him? The one on the right hissed under his breath. "Woz she mean by *rape*? You said we'd jus' scare her."

"Yeah, my ol' lady would kill me if I rape some sweet lil' librarian." The other guy frowned. Everett blinked at the obscure logic of that statement. But maybe his buddy would be the voice of reason for Paul.

Or not.

Paul shuffled his feet and shrugged, clenching his fists and frowning at the floor. He acted every bit an errant child. Caught, yet belligerent enough to refuse to back down. He waved away the objection, swaying as the motion unbalanced him. "We're not gonna rape 'er. Jus' gonna rough her up some. It's upta her how much she wantsa get roughed up."

The other two nodded as if that clarified things.

Betty frowned at the three. "Rough me up? You mean you only came here to hit me?" She placed a hand to her chest, her voice sharp with sarcasm. "I'm so relieved your moral compass draws the line at rape, but leaves you free to assault."

Quit mocking them. Everett gripped a nearby shelf and steeled his nerves as the tension in the room thickened. Betty obviously wasn't a wilting flower. She brandished words like weapons, nicking at their male pride with her sharp wit. And here he was, hiding behind a bookshelf, his brain grappling for words that might halt the ugly progression of this crisis. For Christ's sake, he was Everett Dean, Founding Owner of a multi-trillion dollar company. He had commanded the attention and respect of rooms filled with men more powerful and combative than these three drunks. But that's not what they would see if he stepped out from behind the rows of books. They'd see destitute Clark, the weak-ass homeless guy. Even if Everett could get in a few blows, the three of them would hand him his ass. And Betty would still get raped.

"You...makin' fun of us, bishhh?" Brute Two slurred and scrubbed a hand through his overgrown mullet, as if he didn't quite understand her words or her sarcasm. Too much booze coursing through their bodies to expect logic to win out.

"You needa be taught some manners." Brute One hitched his workingman's jeans up from the thick belt around his waist. "A purty thing like you should know when to keep your mouth shut."

Brute Two grabbed his crotch. "Yeah, and when to open it."

Paul merely chuckled, and fondled his own crotch as if in anticipation.

"So we're back to the topic of rape." Betty sighed like the topic bored her. She might dress like an obedient housewife, but that didn't seem to be her true nature.

Paul snorted. "It's only rape if you don' enjoy it. And I promise you'll be screaming my name." He stumbled toward her.

Betty lifted her eyebrows like a mother detecting a lie, her voice take-no-prisoners firm. "The dictionary is on the shelves at the back wall. I recommend you refine your definition of rape. You're missing a few key points."

Former girlfriends had often labeled Everett a selfish bastard because his priorities had always been Preditech's bottom line and pushing the cybernetic envelope, with his romantic relationships a distant third. But watching three men threaten a woman with physical and sexual assault? Even selfish bastards had to draw a line in the sand, and Everett's was set, bold and immovable, at forcing a woman against her will. Betty's stance was similarly bold and immoveable. She wasn't backing down, even in the face of these threats. Everett donned his CEO arrogance and readied for the battle to come.

The hamster running the wheel which made Paul's brain function finally caught up and Betty's words registered on his frontal cortex. He growled. "Fuck you, bitch."

"Just try it."

Paul lunged. Betty leaned back on the desk and kicked. Her heel swiped his chin, snapping his head to the side so he careened against Brute Two. Brute One grabbed at her, but she bashed his arms away and kneed his stomach. He folded on a grunt and collapsed to the right.

Everett stepped away from the shelves, fists at the ready, looking for where to jump into the fray. But she didn't need his help. Betty fought like this was a staged movie scene, her motions swift and calculated. Her blows precise and effective. For all her '50s housewife style, she was a fucking juggernaut, and he couldn't take his eyes off her.

She ducked Paul's uppercut, jabbing her elbow into his ribs, then whirled for roundhouse kick. Paul keened over, but Brute One grabbed her skirt and she tumbled onto him, landing an elbow into his diaphragm. He curled in with a gasping yowl and she rolled to her knees to bash his temple, knocking him out.

A nearby growl caught Everett's attention right as Brute Two lunged for him. Smart man in spite of his drunken stupor, he'd chosen to attack the weak-ass bystander instead of Betty. Everett jerked back just in time, the incoming blow glancing off the solid wood bookshelf. Brute Two yowled in pain, then turned to lunge again. Everett blocked the wild downward swing and wrapped an arm around the guy's head. If he could subdue the dickhead, maybe he'd give up the fight.

No luck. It was like hugging a greased pig. Brute Two twisted in Everett's grip, swatting at his shoulders and head, fortunately without enough leverage to be effective. But all the squirming turned him around until his face was pressed into the rancid armpit fabric of Everett's shirt. Brute Two's cries were muffled and he clutched at Everett, pushing and pulling alternately but ineffectively to escape what was no doubt a smell more deadly than chloroform. Everett glanced up to make sure Betty was still holding her own.

She was.

Paul threw a cross punch. Betty caught it and rolled with it, bending and tossing him over her shoulders. He tumbled to the floor on a yelp, but clambered back to his feet to face her, panting.

"You think you can beat me? You're just a fucking librarian." He huffed. Even with his nose already broken from a previous altercation and his chin bleeding from where she'd smashed her heel into his face, he maintained his bravado. Damn whatever liquid courage they'd been drinking.

Betty stood and swept the wrinkles from her skirt with practiced nonchalance and shrugged. "True, I am *just* a librarian. But you're an unemployed drunk with no girlfriend. And none of that has any bearing on the fact this librarian still kicked your ass."

The taunt struck home. He feinted, then jabbed. She blocked and twisted as his momentum carried him close, punching the heel of her hand against his already-broken nose. He dropped to the floor like a sack of manure.

Brute Two still struggled in Everett's arms. Poor bastard. He was probably asphyxiating on the stench, but Everett didn't dare release his grip. Instead, he reached for the ceramic planter resting atop a side table and bashed it against Brute Two's head. The planter shattered, raining chunks of yellow porcelain, dirt, and leafy plant onto the floor. Brute Two's body dropped slack, a sudden dead weight that nearly ripped Everett's arm off.

He looked at Betty, who stood amid the two unconscious bodies of her attackers, looking back at him. Her expression of mute shock nearly undid him. Holy shit, what had he done? He blinked and glanced at the rim of the broken planter still in his hands, bloody where he'd smashed it against Brute Two's temple. *Ohmigod he's dead!*

Everett swallowed back the bile rushing up his throat. So much for avoiding the authorities. So much for solving the mystery of who was trying to kill him. So much for defending a woman against would-be rapists. Everett was going to jail, simple as that. No amount of money or influence would save him. *Once a delinquent, always a delinquent.*

He wanted to vomit.

Instead, he stared back at Betty, his heart withering. "Did I… did I kill him?"

Chapter Seven

Betty's hands shook. Her heart hammered in her chest and sweat seeped from every pore. Not because three men had threatened her with rape and she'd had to fight off their attack. But because of the man who stood in front of her, his face ashen white tinged with green and a would-be attacker still dangling from his choke-hold.

Now that he'd cleaned his hair and the grime off his face with the soap she'd given him, she recognized Clark for who he really was: Everett Dean, Founder and CEO of premier cybernetic manufacturer Preditech. The same company whose serial numbers were lasered onto her own CPU, wires, and hardware. The same company that had helped make her what she was today. A cyborg. A secret spy. A tool for dastardly deeds. *Persona non grata* in the opinion of the world. Because of him, the technology existed to make her a cyborg. Because she'd volunteered to be made a cyborg, she'd been used as a tool rather than as a human. Because she'd been used as a tool, she lived in fear of being used as such again.

Fear more potent than any she'd ever known shot icy shards through her veins, cutting so deep she might bleed to death from the emotion. Her heart pounded in her ears, thoughts racing through her head so fast she could barely grasp them.

Everett Dean stood in her library, and if anyone discovered this fact, the world might very well explode.

News of his death had hit all the channels four days ago. Four days after the utter destruction of his private jet in a northern Indiana cornfield, a dirty and sweaty man dressed in designer labels showed up at her library and asked to use the computers. Why fake his own death? Why come to *this* library, when there were numerous others between here and the crash site?

Even if she wasn't the target for his sudden entrance into her life, she wasn't safe with him around. He was both lauded and reviled for his life's work. Considered a genius or an evil villain, depending on who you talked to, although the majority of society leaned toward the latter. If she could recognize him, so could anyone else. And she would get caught in the resulting crossfire.

Nothing good would come of this. Her gut churned, her head spinning with a myriad of horrific ramifications. Her hair-trigger sense of self-preservation screamed *doom*.

Everett Dean was bad juju to have around.

"I'll… I'll help clean up the mess." Everett's shaky voice broke through her swirling emotions. His gaze swiveled between the two bodies at her feet, the body still in his grip, and the broken planter in his trembling hand. He swallowed loudly, as if choking back the contents of his stomach, and swayed slightly.

He was in shock. So was she, but her systems regulated adrenaline when under stress. She would be fine. But if she didn't do something, Everett Dean might pass out in her lobby. Sympathy flooded her heart, damn her soft soul. She could lay the blame for all the wrongs she'd ever experienced as a cyborg at his feet another time. Right now, he needed her help.

She smiled and dismissed the mess with a wave of her hand. "Don't worry, Ev-um-Clark. It's just dirt."

"Oh. That too, but I… I meant the bodies—"

She shook her head and stepped over Paul's prone form. She eased Brute Two out of Everett's grip and let the unconscious man drop to the floor like the trash he was. "Like I said. It's just dirt. They're not a threat to me anymore. Thank you for… your help. But I can handle this from here and you should leave."

"Leave you here alone? With them?" Everett waved his hand to indicate the three unconscious men, his voice a low whisper. "What if they wake up?"

The man who'd publicly been labeled a Heartless Bastard by every woman he'd ever dated was unwilling to leave her, a relative stranger. No one had ever expressed concern for her safety, and Betty floundered for what to do and say, particularly in light of Everett's seemingly uncharacteristic protective streak.

"Well, if they do, I'll give them more of the same." She flashed him a smile she hoped was reassuring even as confusion and uncertainty eddied in her head. She cupped his hand in hers and eased his grip on the ceramic planter shard, brushing off the film of dirt and checking for cuts which might need first-aid.

His minty breath fanned the top of her head while she inspected his hand and his long, capable fingers. The very ones he'd used to design, wire, and solder the prototypes for the cybernetic systems which currently kept her calm and capable of fending off the unwanted advances of three drunks. Her world teetered. She currently held the hands of her own Maker, like holding the hand of God. Even if that god was just a man.

A man who pulled his hand out of hers as if uncomfortable with her inspection. In his defense, he was also a man on the run, so likely uneasy about too much scrutiny. She would react the same if she were in his shoes. She dropped her own hands and looked at him.

He cleared his throat. "Betty, it's obvious you can take care of yourself. But I don't like the thought of you being here alone with these three. What if they wake up and you can't give them more of the same? What if they catch you when you're distracted? What if... I dunno, what if they lie about what actually happened? Wouldn't it be better if I..."

His voice trailed off and he glanced away, his shoulder dropping in defeat. He chuckled to himself. "Never mind. A homeless person wouldn't be much of a character reference for you if it came to that."

Betty's voice strained against the sudden tightness in her throat. In a matter of one plane crash, Everett had gone from being on top of the world to a man on the run. A penniless vagabond with no power or respect. Many people might be thrilled with how far the mighty Everett Dean had fallen. She was conflicted about the influence his work had on her life, but Betty could not muster any joy in another's misfortune.

"Clark, please don't worry about me. I'm going to call an officer friend to take care of these three. But unless you want to get stuck answering his questions, I suggest you exit out the back door." As she expected, panic flashed in his eyes at the mention of getting the police involved. He didn't balk when she ushered him back to the computers. "Did you find what you'd been searching for? On the computer?"

His face screwed up in confusion, no doubt by her sudden change of topic. "Uh, not all of it. I'll need to come back, if it's okay with you."

Her librarian smile settled into place. "Of course. We're open to serve the public, and that includes you."

In the time it would take Detective Grady to arrive, Everett could be well away from the building and safe if he moved quickly. Which he seemed inclined to do, and she heard the back door click closed before she had walked to her desk and dialed the phone. Detective Grady had a crush on her, which she tried not to encourage because she wasn't attracted to him, and because she didn't want him digging into her past. He might unearth things he shouldn't. Like the fact she hadn't always been Betty Hayworth, or the fact she was a cyborg.

But current circumstances required a more official deterrent than she could provide without undo force.

As she waited for Detective Grady to arrive, she stared at the three men still comatose in the library entryway. She should worry about them, considering the fact serious injury or alcohol poisoning were possibilities. But she didn't. She must have spent all her sympathy on Everett Dean. These three could suffer with the consequences of their own poor decisions. Lord knows life had forced her to do so.

She had volunteered to have cybernetic parts implanted in her body, but she'd been sold a rotten bill of goods. She'd been told lies. Lies about serving her country and rooting out evil and making the world a better place, when in reality she'd merely slept with powerful people to gather blackmail intel. At least, that's what she assumed she'd done as a spy; those assignments were many of the missing memories.

Not knowing what she'd actually done as an escort/spy was probably a blessing. But that didn't negate the fact she'd likely done vile things in her country's service. And karma kept rearing her ugly head in her life, a constant punishment for having made such monumentally stupid choices. For merely having the audacity to exist at all, it sometimes seemed. Like now.

Was this what was happening with Everett? Was karma coming home to roost for his past mistakes? Everett Dean wasn't the agent who had recruited Betty. And he hopefully had not intended his cybernetic systems to be used to spy on his own country. But Everett Dean *was* the cyborg industry. Its founding father, its face to the public, its mascot. All the wrongs she had ever experienced as a cyborg she'd always summarily laid at his feet.

But she could no longer muster that blame. Couldn't find the hate it required to be happy in his misery. Her own cup of misery had overflowed. She wouldn't wish that on anyone else, least of all a man who had been brave enough to help her without being asked to. Everett had fought and subdued the third attacker. Had come to her aid. She couldn't recollect another time anyone had tried to intervene on her behalf or put themselves in harm's way to protect her. Even though she was perfectly capable of protecting herself, he'd still stepped up against one of her attackers. Just like the alpha male heroes from her romance books.

That had to count for something, right?

Grady arrived right as the three began to revive. Betty explained briefly what had happened, leaving out pertinent details such as her advanced fighting skills and anything that might pique his interest in Everett.

"Well, boys. I could take you downtown if Miz Betty wants to press charges." Grady rocked back on his heels, his thumbs hooked on a belt loop, dragging the waistline of his pants down so his paunch protruded further. The southern twang he affected scraped against her nerves like chewing on wool. His show of machismo was why she'd called him, and the two friends seemed adequately cowered by it. Paul the Total Asshole, however, speared her with a bleary glare, his lips tight in a mulish line. Or was that a pout?

Before he could spout more garbage, she held up a hand to stop him. "If I press assault charges, the arrest will show on your record. You'll never find legitimate employment again."

"Yup." Grady nodded his glistening bald head and clucked his tongue. "Potential employers will drop you like a turd on fire."

Wrong image. Well, actually, a fairly accurate imagery, but not one she would have used. Total Asshole glanced toward the floor, his expression beneath the blood and additional bruising nearly resembled regret. Was he sobering up? Did he realize what he'd threatened to do? Was it possible he might feel remorse?

Grady continued as he pointed the three men toward the front door and swaggered in that direction with them. "Any of you boys come 'round here bothering Miz Betty again, you'll get a pair of metal bracelets instead of a warning."

"Hey, what about the homeless guy who attacked me?" The one with the mullet piped up. "Shouldn't you be all up in his ass, too?"

"Oh, this ain't me all up in your ass." Grady practically snapped his own neck, whirling to assert his authority on the drunk. "If I was all up in your ass, you'd taste it."

"The homeless guy who attacked you?" Betty crossed her arms and speared Mullet Man with a raised eyebrow. "Oh, you mean the library patron who came to my aid to fend off the aggressive and unwanted assault by you three?"

"Fucker stunk like a dumpster! That amount of BO should be against the law!"

"And you stink like a bottle of rotgut." Betty snapped at him, riled with a weird sense of protectiveness for Everett from the insult. "You have no room by which to judge anyone else."

Before she punctuated her words by stomping over and ripping off the man's face, Grady waved her away and shoved the three men out the door. "You boys better git before I haul you in just for shits and giggles."

The three men stumbled down the steps to the sidewalk, grumbling and shooting irritated glances over their shoulders. But they didn't mouth off again, merely continued down the road away from the library.

Betty struggled to rein in her emotions as Grady shut the door with a gentle *click* that contrasted the fury pounding in her chest. If she didn't get a handle on her murderous rage, she risked exposing her cybernetic enhancements to an officer of the law. That would be bad. *She'd* wind up with a pair of metal bracelets instead of the assholes. And if she was in jail, she wouldn't get to see Everett. You know, to thank him for his help. Not… not for any other reason, surely.

"Detective Grady, thank you for—"

"I'm more than happy to come to your aid whenever you need it, Miz Betty. But I sure wish you'd called before they attacked."

Her anger iced over at Grady's condescending words. She hated when he called her Miz Betty, especially when he said it with that southern drawl. His affected use of the title came off as more patronizing than respectful. She clasped her hands at her waist to refrain from punching him for his dismissive comment and forced what she hoped was a reasonable tone. "Detective Grady, it's not like they gave me fair warning. If I'd tried to call, they would have overpowered me before I could relay the necessary information to the 911 operator, and I'd be raped and probably beaten right now, with the authorities none the wiser."

"Panic buttons are cheap and easy to install. Surely the library budget has room for—"

She shook her head and chuckled. "Yes, there's room in the budget for the button, but not for the charges we'd incur from all the false alarms. Children patronize this library as well. They're quick as lightning, and nothing is safe from their curious little fingers. Trust me, I speak from experience."

"Don't let it worry you none. It's my job to be concerned for your safety." Grady buried his hands in his front pockets and cleared his throat as he rocked back on his heels. "I think you already know, the matter of your safety is a rather personal issue for me."

She knew. Knew and tried not to encourage his attention or behave in a manner he could translate as anything more than the same polite civility she used with librarian patrons. "I appreciate your concern, Detective. But you're not my bodyguard, and neither should I expect you to behave as such. A woman should be proactive in her personal safety, and that's why I take self-defense classes—"

"Self-defense classes give you a false sense of security. You simply can't hold your own against a man." Grady jangled the change in his pocket. "You're just a little thing, a single woman who works and lives alone. And you dress to show off your figure. Hate to say it, but it's almost like you're asking for trouble."

Aaaaand, this was why she'd never date Detective Grady. Well, this, and the fact he might learn she was a cyborg. Injured first responders had been the alpha phase of cybernetic implants, and it hadn't gone over well with the public or the other first responders. Grady had once hinted about losing a partner in the past to that program. His tone had been all she'd needed to understand which side of the cyborg coin his opinions lay.

Betty made a show of peering down at her soft pink gingham dress which fell to the middle of her calves, and buttoned up to a few fingers beneath her throat. Between the three-quarter-length sleeves and her gloves, a mere few inches of her arms were uncovered. She could hardly be more modestly dressed if she wore a church choir robe.

Drawing in a deep breath, she looked up at Grady and held his gaze so he would not mistake her words for anything but the verbal stiff-arm they were. "Again, I appreciate your concern, Detective. However, it's the twenty-second century and all the points you enumerated are tragically outdated concepts. My marital status and lifestyle choices are no different than yours, yet you don't seem to be concerned for your own safety. And my clothing is no more revealing than yours. I dress this way because it pleases me, and for no other reason."

He held his hands up to calm her. The stance only served to do the opposite. If the jerk called her *darlin'*, she would hit him. "Miz Betty, I only mean that you're a beautiful woman and men can't help themselves around someone like you. You're bound to attract the wrong kind of attention because—"

"I'm sorry your own gender has such a lack of self-control." And people thought *she* promoted an outdated era because of her clothing choices. Grady lived and breathed those archaic stereotypes. Betty couldn't take any more. She yanked the library door open in the unmistakable invitation for Grady to leave. "You obviously believe I encouraged the attack today by the sheer fact that I have a vagina. From now on, I'll be sure to leave it at home. Good day, Detective."

Chapter Eight

From the safety of a shade tree across the street, Everett watched the plainclothes officer leave the library. The man stomped to his car, face red and mottled as if angry about something. Maybe he was enraged by the attack on Betty, but Everett didn't think so. The three drunks had skittered down the street with too little supervision by the detective. How could he be sure they weren't hiding, waiting for a chance to have another go at it? And too much time had passed between the drunks leaving and the detective's own departure. He and Betty had had time to talk.

What could they have discussed that had made the detective so irate?

During the brief bit of time Everett had spent with Betty, she'd been nothing but gracious, generous, and accommodating. Until threatened with rape. Then she'd become downright brazen. He admired her wit and backbone. Plus, she had taken out two men as easily as waving good-bye, and still had the presence of mind to be concerned for his safety where the police were concerned. Doubtful they'd take kindly to a homeless person attacking a citizen, especially a homeless person who was actually Preditech's supposedly dead CEO, not that Betty knew.

Although his own self-preservation demanded he hightail it away from the library, the action smacked of cowardice. Some tiny shrapnel of morality berated Everett for leaving Betty alone with three guys who had made their nefarious intentions clear. Even if they were unconscious and she was more than capable of self-defense. Now that the three had scurried down the street like the vermin they were, and the officer had also left, Everett wanted to return to the library to make sure Betty was okay. But what would he do if she wasn't? Because there was no way she was. What woman would be okay after such an ordeal? Everett still shook from the altercation, and he'd recently survived an attempt on his life in the form of a fiery plane crash. Betty was no doubt curled in a corner somewhere, sobbing and reliving the attack on an endless mental loop.

And he thought offering a few awkward words of comfort would help? He was as delusional as those three guys.

Besides, she likely had an emotional support system of friends who would comfort her more effectively than he ever could. And he had bigger problems than the emotional state of a person he'd met mere hours ago. He had a life and company to get back to. And, more immediately, he had to find a place to tuck in for the night. The excuses were flimsy, and settled like rocks in the back of his throat. He was a jackass for walking away from her, even though she doubtfully needed whatever lame help he could offer. But he was a selfish bastard and self-preservation ruled the day.

Everett hitched his satchel on his shoulder and headed in the general direction of where he assumed the river's homeless camp would be. Finding a place to rest for the evening was easier said than done. All the spots along the river bank and under the shade of trees were already claimed by others, and Everett spent the evening skirting the most obvious encampments, tromping through the others, and apologizing at every turn.

"You're new to this, ain't ya?" An older man piped up as Everett once again crossed the wrong line. He glanced down, considering his own filthy clothes from the old man's perspective. He looked every bit like some down-on-his-luck bougie douche. Like his wife had kicked him out of the house for not buying the right kind of tapered candles. He didn't fit in with the crowd around here. He was as much an outsider here as he had been within the Chicago social circles.

"Uh, yeah. It's pretty obvious, isn't it? Sorry, I just"—he wobbled as another person flinched away and glared at him—"I'm not familiar with where all the invisible lines of demarcation are."

"Demarcation?"

"What's claimed and what isn't. Look, I'm passing through. Here for a few days before I move on. I'm not trying to infringe on anyone's territory, just trying to find a place to sleep."

The old man squinted at him through a snarled mane of hair and beard. "You ain't a cop, are ya? Or someone's gonna cause trouble? We don't need none of that 'round here."

"No sir, I'm not. I don't need any of that either." Everett scratched at his four-day stubble.

"Sir?" The old man smacked his gums. "Ain't been called sir in a long while. Most people call me Gramps."

Everett chuckled. "I guess Betty from the library is rubbing off on me. She's the one who suggested I might find a spot in this area."

Delight lit Gramps's bloodshot eyes. "Betty, you say? Miz Hayworth? That sweet angel comes along every winter with warm clothes and hot chocolate. She could charm the pants off the devil."

The battle scene at the library still fresh in his mind, Everett laughed. "If she didn't knock him out first."

"Can't imagine her being so ornery. More'n likely, she'd smother him with homemade brownies." A hoarse cackle sounded from Gramps's throat and he slapped his knees. Everett was tempted to tell the old man how Betty could kick ass like an assassin, but he chuckled instead. After all, his backpack currently held a homemade brownie, courtesy of one lovely, enigmatic Miz Hayworth.

As if Everett had passed some test, Gramps jerked his chin to the left. "Rest your head over there. Mind you, it's just for a few nights, and you best not be invitin' any trouble with the law."

"Not at all. I assure you that's the last thing I want." Everett swung his pack off his shoulder to dig past the parachute he'd shoved in it, wishing he had money. He'd been a generous tipper in Chicago, and this man had been more helpful than most doormen—Everett could open his own doors, thank you very much, but finding a place to sleep apparently eluded him. Antony hadn't packed any cash, only a few meager rations Everett had already eaten, band aids, sunscreen, bug repellent, and a burner phone he couldn't use because he had no one to call who didn't assume he was dead.

Smiling at the bit of irony it represented, Everett pulled out the wrapped dessert he'd saved from lunch. Betty had *dropped* so much food on his plate, he'd been too full to be smothered by her homemade brownie. It would have made a tasty dinner, but would now serve a higher purpose than satisfying his sweet tooth.

"I appreciate your kindness, Gramps." Even as his stomach grumbled, Everett handed the treat to the man. "This isn't much in the form of payment, but I hope you enjoy it. Miz Hayworth made it."

Watching a young child opening gifts at Christmas couldn't possibly compare to the delight which lit the old man's face when he pulled back the napkin. It reminded Everett of the gifts he'd been given and had given in his lifetime. He hated the reminder. Unlike this brownie, all of those gifts had come with strings attached.

Gramps smiled a gap-toothed grin filled with chocolatey goodness as Everett settled into a corner by a hefty tree root. He pulled the parachute out of his pack to use as ground cover, and tucked his satchel behind his head for a makeshift pillow.

The August evening remained warm and humid, but he ignored the sweat trickling down his temples and throat and pooling at his back. That particular sensation had become a constant companion these last few days, but was no match for the thoughts swirling in his brain as the evening eased to night. He closed his eyes and reflected on what his research had unearthed.

Every gambler knows the house has the edge on odds. Everett had deluded himself Preditech had been the *house*. That his company had been a safe bet. That he'd been the one calling the shots. Shoulda realized DCO had bankrolled everyone all this time, and was now calling in their markers.

And Everett's senior staff? They'd encouraged it, because it would pad their paychecks. According to their intra-company emails, his staff had no moral qualms about being rolled into the DCO. They were just happy to keep their jobs. In fact, if the company emails were any indication, they hadn't spared Everett a thought. And the few thoughts spared weren't flattering to their former CEO.

Unless he came forth to prove he wasn't dead and thus make himself a target for a second murder attempt, everything that had once been his would get ripped and torn and manhandled and passed around to the salivating vultures. No matter what action he would or would not take, he was going to lose his life, either his literal life or the life he'd forged from the beginning days spent in his lab. If he did manage to stay alive, he'd have to lay low and stick to the edge of society. Stay unknown. On the down-low. Unnoticed. A nobody.

Pretty much his current situation.

Everett's heart sank and bitterness crawled to his stomach where it churned like the morning after a drunken bender. Most of his senior staff had been with him since the beginning. It shouldn't be such a gut punch that the men and women who had helped him shape his company would care so little about his legacy. They were so concerned about their meal ticket, they were eager to throw him under the bus without losing a moment's sleep over it.

Maybe he wasn't the only selfish bastard around. He'd certainly surrounded himself with them. Birds of a feather, and all that.

But Antony hadn't been selfish. He'd risked and lost his life trying to keep Everett safe. And Betty was the epitome of selflessness. She didn't know it, but she'd risked losing her job and social standing as a respectable citizen by helping him avoid the police.

What had he lost in all of this?

Everything.

"You carry a heavy weight on them shoulders, boy." Gramps jarred Everett from his morose thoughts.

He glanced at the man, lounging against the tree as if he hadn't a worry in the world, not even the worry for where his next meal would come from. The older man smiled, the wrinkles around his eyes bunching up so he squinted. Everett shrugged. "Yeah, I got a lot on my mind."

Gramps huffed a laughed which morphed into a brief wheezing-coughing spell. He shook his head. "Any worries that drag you down like that ain't worth the effort. Look at that Atlas guy, carrying the weight of the world. Where'd it get him?"

Everett knew little about Greek mythology, but understood how Atlas felt, straining to keep from being crushed by his burden. Had the other gods taken credit for his efforts? Had they claimed his successes for themselves?

Gramps leaned toward Everett as if to reveal a secret. "Boy, you need to get yourself a good woman. She'll help you carry those burdens so they feel like they ain't even there."

Everett nearly choked. A good woman? That was Gramps's secret to a happy life? "And you know this from personal experience, do you?"

"Sure do. Long time ago, before I got to where I am today, I had me a good woman." Gramps stared off at a distant memory, his smile soft and wistful. "Find a good woman and treat her right, respect her, and let 'er shine. Ya gotta give her room to shine; you can't smother her. Your arms gotta be both strong and soft when she falls into 'em. And she's gotta trust that you got her back. Then she'll move mountains for ya."

"Not like they're growing on trees." Everett's snort was louder than he'd intended. "You talk like I can go to the store and pluck one off the shelf."

Gramps snorted in return. "Course you can't. That's why they're so special. Ya gotta earn them. Every day." Gramps slanted Everett a sly wink. "Miz Hayworth'd be one of the good ones for the man who deserves 'er."

Everett nodded, images of Betty wandering through his mind. Betty, head held high, facing off against three aggressive drunks. Betty staring at his hand like it was a delicate rose petal. Betty handing him a plateful piled with food and apologizing for the meager selection. Yeah, she'd be a good woman for a man who deserved her. A strong, capable man who could protect her and stand beside her and love her without reservation. Too bad Everett wasn't that man. Had never been that man, even before the plane crash.

Still, thoughts of Betty were far more pleasant than thoughts of betrayal and threats on his life.

He settled more comfortably into his makeshift bed, crossing his arms around the satchel behind his head, and stared at the night's skyglow through the leaves of the tree as a sultry breeze danced through the branches. His imagination grew wings, offering delectable thoughts of Betty. Was she safe at home? Was she calm and peaceful after the day's crises? Maybe she sat out on her balcony, gazing up at the same night sky, sipping a chilled glass of wine and fanning the humid air away from the damp skin of her neck and bare shoulders. Alone at home, she would wear a white cotton nightgown, its simplistic design both chaste is its virginal quality and utterly seductive in what its fabric barely concealed. It would rest along her curves as both an invitation and an obstacle. Her lips would be the gatekeeper, either firm and unyielding or soft, slightly parted, eager for a kiss.

How he wanted to pulled her into his arms and kiss her like a man who'd earned the right to plunder that paradise.

But he wasn't.

The knowledge should have kept him awake. Should have stopped his wistful thoughts of Betty. But the distant buzz of Greater Broad Ripple's night life and droning din of what the old man had called the Seven-Year Cicadas added a hypnotic cacophony lulling him into a fitful sleep. He dreamed of Betty. Sweet and lovely and laughing. Carefree and teasing. On her back with her hair splayed around her, reaching for him, her eyes sparkling like diamonds. His dreams grew dark and tormented. The image of Betty overlaid with the foreboding view of Antony's emotionless red-eyes and the screams of sirens. Everett jerked awake in the early dawn, panting and sweating, the vision of a cyborg Betty gone rogue imprinted on his brain long after the haze of slumber had lifted.

Chapter Nine

"**L**ook, Mommy. I'm a thyborg dinothaur. *Pew! Pew! Rawhr!*"

An adorable six-year-old boy with a missing front tooth and the resulting lisp waved an arm wrapped in construction paper. He stomped around the room growling a stream of *pew-pews* punctuated with roars at the other children enjoying this morning's Toddler Time activities. Most children ignored him, but a few squealed at the exciting new game and followed suit, streaking paper with colorful lines no doubt meant to be cybernetic wiring, and taping it around their arms and legs.

Betty bit her lips to keep from laughing at their antics. She also refrained from pointing out the fact dinosaurs weren't cyborgs, and cyborgs weren't equipped with weaponry.

The mothers were simply horrified.

"Conor! Stop that at once!" Conor's mother gasped in mortification, gaze darting to the other mothers as if to gauge their reaction to her son's unacceptable behavior. "Miss Betty doesn't want you running around her library, pretending to be one of those horrid creatures."

Was Mrs. Murphy referring to the dinosaur or the cyborg

portion of Conor's play acting? What would she say if she knew Betty was one of those *horrid creatures*?

"Mrs. Murphy, I don't mind." Betty ignored the dual pang of resentment and fear, and laughed as Conor swung his makeshift cybernetic appendage in her direction with a *Pew-pew.* She clutched her side on an exaggerated groan of pain as the imaginary laser hit its mark. The little boy jumped in delight and continued to other victims.

Betty turned back to Mrs. Murphy. "Unless it's physically unsafe for your son or the other children, I'm happy to let them explore their imaginations."

Another mother scoffed as she sipped her pricey designer brand coffee. "I wouldn't want my child imitating such an aberration any more than I'd want him pretending to be a criminal or a bum. Those things are a menace—"

Her own child ran past, a paper of colorful "circuitry" taped around his head, shouting triumphant *pew-pews,* effectively cutting short her tirade. The dark-haired boy turned to Betty. "I'm Captain of the cyborgs. We're fighting alien invaders!"

"Well, may the Force be with you, Captain." Betty saluted, humor bubbling in her heart. She planned each Toddler Time event with meticulous attention to detail, yet the children always derailed it in the most delightful way. Leave it up to the antics of the innocent to make these moms eat their own words.

"Miss Betty, why do you encourage such behavior?" The first mother admonished Betty as if she was encouraging the children to join a crime syndicate.

"Karen, don't blame Miss Betty." Another mom, whose two-year-old daughter placed stickers with painstaking precision on her hands instead of the intended paper bag craft, addressed Mrs. Murphy. "She read the book *Natalie Names Her Emotions* and chose activities to go with it. She couldn't have known Conor would make a cyborg arm out of the construction paper."

Betty smiled at the show of support.

Mrs. Murphy demurred to Betty. "Well, perhaps next time, you should choose activities which don't offer materials children might misuse."

Swallowing the retort that burned the back of her throat, Betty dipped her head and demurred in return. "I'll take you suggestion under advisement."

"Don't blame the children." Another mother spoke up. "The news is twenty-four-seven about Everett Dean's plane crash and what that means to the cyborg industry. It's impossible to escape it."

"I'm glad Everett Dean crashed and burned. He and his cyborg industry have been nothing but a public nightmare since he started it." The Cyborg Captain's mother spoke as if Everett Dean was an absent baby daddy delinquent on child support. Her ugly vehemence was all too common where anything cyborg was concerned. Betty grit her teeth against her rising agitation. As a cyborg, she had to toe a razor's edge in a conversation such as this one. This was a systemic loathing they espoused. A unifying hatred, cutting across gender, race, socioeconomic status, and educational level. Cyborgs were the common enemy everyone could rally behind, like the Nazis of WWII. And while the war raged on, Betty struggled to avoid all the shots fired at her kind.

Her gut churned at the bitter pill. Wouldn't these mothers implode if they knew Everett Dean had been in this library yesterday? Would they cease their rhetoric if they knew what Betty had learned from following his internet search yesterday? Would it give them even a moment's pause?

She sighed. Probably not. But she'd spent a sleepless night contemplating it.

Yesterday, after Detective Grady had stomped away like a child denied a treat, she had locked the library door for the night, then had beelined for the computers. She needed to know what Everett had searched on the computer all day. The house of cards which was her life threatened to topple from the day's head-spinning new developments. So many emotions had ping-ponged through her heart. So many revelations. She was desperate to grasp at anything to keep it all from collapsing, as if knowing what Everett searched online would do anything but crush her world. Still, she was a moth to a flame, unable to stop or even slow her next actions.

"Please let it be porn." She murmured as she slid off her left glove and eased her cybernetic finger jack into the computer port. Data surged into the CPU part of her brain, a disturbing, blistering sensation as she sorted through the bombardment of digital zeros and ones, decoding them, following the faint trail Everett had tried to cover. Without her cybernetic brain, she might have lost his trail a few steps in. He had dusted his tracks well, but not enough shake her. like a cat hunting a mouse—wrong image; like a bloodhound—she followed as he leaped, backtracked, and zig-zagged.

Instead of finding porn, or even proof he was responsible for all that was wrong in the world, her discovery was far more unsettling. Government greed, apathetic employees, a feeding frenzy of a social network, and an utter absence of family and friends. Everett was a man alone and up against hellish adversaries.

Sadly, she knew this same isolation. Was Everett as much a pawn as she in a game neither wanted to play? Wait, was she actually empathizing with the man who was part of the reason she was a cyborg? Damn her kind heart.

Betty retracted her jack and slumped back in the chair and rubbed her temples. She chuckled without humor. Had it only been a few days ago when she'd lamented her monotonous existence and craved companionship? This wasn't what she'd had in mind. Nothing about this situation could turn out in her favor. Her luck always ran sour. Why should this be any different? Sticking around, being anywhere near Everett, was certain to upend her life and put her in harm's way. But—

Pfft. There was always a *but,* wasn't there?

But, she couldn't stay away from him. Morbid curiosity, maybe. Womanly attraction, possibly. Her bleeding heart, definitely. Not to mention her apparent lack of any sense of self-preservation, because a sane person would turn their backs and run like mad. Yet she couldn't fight the soul-deep feeling that if something bad happened to Everett, being a cyborg would be a thousand times more dangerous than it was now.

Because Everett Dean was the biggest supporter of cybernetic individuals, right? He had to be. He was the reason the industry even existed. He had taken the concept of mere prosthetics and elevated it to an artform—*A Better You,* according to Preditech's marketing campaigns—where the individual could still appear 100 percent human but have almost superhero-like abilities, such as her combat skills and her computer-jack finger.

Was it his fault his creation had been twisted into something ugly?

The urge to stick around and help Everett was there, cementing in her muscles and fusing with her determination. As if aiding him through his current crisis, whatever it was, would wash away all of her own sins as well.

"Once bitten, twice shy." She had muttered the world-weary phrase, but the words had echoed empty, even in the cozy library. "Oh, honey. You've been bitten so many times by life, you're practically a chew toy at this point."

Clarity had hit her like an uppercut. She was going to help Everett Dean.

With her newfound mission still in place, she couldn't allow the Toddler Time mothers to spew cyborg hatred. At least, she had to encourage some semblance of rational thought.

She steeled her nerves and turned to the Captain Cyborg's mother. "You might not like what he represents, but Everett Dean's trailblazing advances in cybernetics have served to revolutionize other industries as well. The medical and prosthetics industry most especially. Anyone receiving a pacemaker or a knee replacement during the last decade has Everett Dean to thank for the quality of their prosthetic and care."

The mothers stared at her like she'd spouted gibberish. One shrugged. "Someone else would have made those advancements eventually. And without creating monsters while doing it."

Betty ground her molars and fought the urge to roll her eyes. She refused to be as dismissive as they were. It would help nothing. "Possibly, Mrs. Mbanu. But would you look a paraplegic in the eye and tell them you wish they were still bound to a wheelchair because you don't like the man who inspired their exoskeletal technology?"

Mrs. Mbanu pursed in her lips in quiet denial. The other mothers glanced around, as if hoping one of them was brave enough to offer an opposing argument. Betty looked at them all in turn. "If someone jumped in front of your self-driving car, and it was unable to react in time to avoid running them over, would you demonize the entire transportation industry, including the person who designed it?"

That either shut them up or marked Betty as a deplorable cyborg sympathizer. Several sets of eyes blinked at her. Unfortunately, the mothers recovered quickly enough.

"The real problem is you don't know who is a cyborg until it's already too late." A mom bobbing a drooling four-month-old on her knee spoke. "One minute, they look like you and me, and the next, they go on a murdering spree. Like the one up in Chicago last week."

Betty bit back a deep sigh. So much for redirecting. A collective affirmation of shock and outrage issued from the other mothers, who talked among themselves in breathless, conspiratorial tones while their precious children cavorted around wearing paper cyborg limbs and shooting imaginary lasers at each other.

Yes, the scene the mothers gossiped about had been awful. And plastered in real-time on all social media and news feeds. Like something straight from a Hollywood movie, what appeared to be a cyborg-gone-rogue had rampaged through a busy city street in Chicago, crumpling cars like foil and threatening the lives of the people inside them. The scene had turned from horrible to heart-breaking when the police had finally gunned down the cyborg until he was nothing more than a lump of wires and bloody flesh.

Betty wasn't new to the gruesome side of life, but this had been broadcast in broad daylight on every multistory building with a public news screen exterior. The details had been visible in hi-definition from blocks away like a kiss-cam on a jumbotron. No one could have missed the raw terror of a cyborg shot with enough bullets to end a world war. No one should have missed the fact the victim had not physically harmed any humans, only vehicles.

Yet they did, focusing instead on the fact the crime had been perpetrated by a cyborg. As if cyborgs were, by their sheer existence, more of a threat to public safety than drugs, terrorists, and viral pandemics combined.

His death had been played to a soundtrack of cheers from the viewing public.

Was this the fate awaiting Betty if she got out of line? No effort had been made to subdue the cyborg or talk him down. The officers on the scene had gone straight from shouting at him to shooting him. If she misbehaved, is this be how the authorities would deal with her?

"You know, it's too bad that cyborg wasn't like a self-driving car." Mrs. Murphy commented loudly enough for all to hear. "Or he could have been remotely disabled instead of shot." She smirked at Betty over the top of her coffee, as if she'd caught

Betty with her hand in the cyborg sympathizer cookie jar. As if Betty supported *those vile creatures.*

Oh, how she wanted to smack the smirk off Mrs. Murphy's face. Betty's previous need for human interaction was sufficiently cured by now.

Betty gave Mrs. Murphy her best *shut the hell up* smile. She addressed the group. "Ladies, our time is almost up today. I appreciate everyone coming to Toddler Time and I hope these programs illustrate how knowledge helps us all combat ignorance and misconception. Next month, we'll take our emotion lesson one step further and cover empathy. I'm sure the kiddos will enjoy the planned activities. They'll involve"—she cupped her mouth as if to whisper a secret, but spoke loud and clear for all the children to hear—"cookies."

The mothers groaned as the children cheered at the sugary promise. It was a dirty trick on Betty's part, and she wasn't a bit sorry for it.

In truth, the activities for next month's Toddler Time didn't involve cookies or revolve around the topic of empathy. Well, they hadn't until thirty seconds ago when Betty had made the entire thing up. But she would figure out a way to make it happen, if only out of churlish spite for the narrow-mindedness of these mothers. And if Conor managed to chew his cookie into the shape of something Mrs. Murphy didn't approve of, well that was too bad.

While the mothers and children finished and packed up to leave, Conor approached Betty. "What's wrong, hon?" She kneeled down to his eye level, noting the tears shimmering in his eyes and the adorable pout of his bottom lip.

"Mith Betty, did I really hurt you with my thyborg arm?"

"No, I'm a pretty tough old bird." She chuckled and squeezed his non-cyborg shoulder. "But if it makes you feel better, maybe you could reprogram your cybernetic arm so it heals instead of hurts."

"You can do that?" His eyes grew wide with awe.

Betty chuckled. "Well *I* can't. I'm only a librarian. But smart people, like Everett Dean who invented cyborgs, probably could. And I have no doubt you are a very smart person, too."

"I *am* thmart!" Excitement lit his hazel eyes and he *beep-boop-booped* his fingers across the colored paper covering his arm. "All done! Now I can heal you."

He waved his arm along her side, buzzing his lips together. She gasped in surprise. "Wow, I'm all better now! Thank you!"

The smile which spread across his face was priceless, like he'd saved the world. He skipped to his mom. "Look, mommy! I'm like Emmett Bean! I'm a good thyborg dinothaur!"

Betty turned her attention to straightening the craft supplies. Wouldn't want it too obvious how much she enjoyed watching Mrs. Murphy seethe from those words, and her son so wonderfully oblivious to his mother's opinions on the matter. If only Conor could always be so. Sadly, his vivid imagination and sweet innocence would eventually give way under the onslaught society's narrow-minded influence. As the years progress, he would likely become yet another cyborg-hater.

In a breath, Betty's smile faltered. Sure, she could find fault with the parenting choices of Mrs. Murphy and the other Toddler Time mothers, but didn't that make her equally as prejudiced? And who was she to judge a parent, having never been one herself. She had failed in so many aspects over the years, but failing to nourish her unborn child was the most painful one. She had cried an ocean of tears for her own fetus who'd never had the chance to be a carefree four-year-old. Yet each time the memory rose again, it brought fresh tears. She blinked them back and swallowed past the painful lump. Crying wouldn't bring her baby back, and neither was it appropriate for Toddler Time and the barracudas known as the Broad Ripple mothers who circled the room hunting for trouble to churn.

By sheer will, Betty managed to hold back the flood until all the participants had moseyed out of the library. A few children even checked out books, which both thrilled and annoyed. Of all the days she wanted an empty building to herself, she had customers who chose to linger and enjoy the benefits their local library offered. When the final mother with child in tow waved good-bye and closed the door, Betty marched to her favorite loveseat and settled on the edge, clutching the arms and leaning her head back to glare at the ceiling. She wanted to curl up and sob herself dry, like she had so many times before even though it resolved nothing. But what if someone entered? What if Everett returned? This was neither the time nor the place to have a cathartic cry.

She couldn't allow salty tears to wash away her regrets, not that they ever truly disappeared. There were too many, and they were wrapped too tightly around her heart, like emotional blood vessels extracting joy. So many poor choices that had hurt others and had only brought her pain and anguish.

Running away from home because she thought she knew more than her mother. Refusing to return and make amends until it was too late to retract all the horrible things she'd said as a rebellious youth. Latching on to men who promised safety and food with hollow declarations of love. Believing that tenuous level of subsistence was enough to nourish the child in her womb. Grasping at the assurances of those who offered her a new life in the service of this great country. Realizing her assignments made her no better than a whore, even though she could not remember the details. Trusting the rhetoric and lies everyone lobbed at her, only to once again end up alone with nothing, like she'd been her entire adult life.

She closed her eyes and inhaled deeply, slowly, her breaths hitching around the knot in her throat. She blinked against the moisture in her eyes, hoping her body would redirect it down the proper ducts instead of allowing it to overflow down her cheeks. Willed away the anguish in her heart as if it were that easy to get rid of. Searched for her center and any kernel of inner strength she could grasp. When her lungs were full to bursting, she exhaled slowly, hating its tremulous quality for the weakness it showed. She swallowed the mucus pooling at the back of her throat—she was an ugly crier—and began the process again.

These Pranayama breathing exercises were meant to calm her swirling emotions. If only her cybernetic systems could regulate heartache like they did adrenaline. Several minutes focused on her breathing should bring her emotions in check so she was better equipped to handle whatever the day could bring her. *Should* being the operative word, but after a couple dozen breaths, she was still no better.

"Betty? Are you okay?" Everett's worried voice pierced her concentration. Her eyes snapped open to see him standing in front of her, his face a mask of panic. Typical man, freaked out about a distraught woman. A bitter chuckle rolled up her throat. He would bolt if she really turned on the water works. Maybe even leave her alone for good. Wouldn't that be best for her tenuous Zen? Before she could answer her own question, he kneeled in front of her and looked up, hands reaching out before he caught himself and pulled them back.

"Betty, what can I do to help you? Should I count your breaths for you? Call someone? Hold your hand? How can I best offer you comfort?"

He didn't ask what was wrong. Didn't point out the water still rimming her eyes, or comment on how mottled and puffy her face likely was. Didn't even touch her without her permission. He merely wanted to be of service.

His behavior was unlike the alpha heroes in her books. Those fictional men were always action-driven. Commanding, domineering, comfortable with making decisions and solving issues. Everett did none of this. Merely waited for her to ask for help, to tell him what she needed. Or not, if that was her decision.

Had anyone ever so selflessly offered themselves in service to her? Former lovers and even the cyborg program recruiters had only talked about what she had to offer them. Her library patrons expected a high degree of service from her. Even Detective Grady made his role as community servant seem like he was doing her a favor by deterring three antagonistic drunks. But Everett, a man who was as down on his luck as humanly possible, extended her comfort and support in whatever manner she needed.

His offer overturned the power dynamic she was accustomed to and it unnerved her already-agitated emotional state. Serving others brought her its own form of power when it was her choice to provide it. Betty lived it every day, helping library patrons and homeless individuals. Being placed in the position of receiving help instead of offering it… that tilted her world on its axis and she shot to a stand.

"Thanks, but I'm okay, Ev-um-Clark." Her hands trembled as she wiped at her eyes and fixed the areas where her makeup had no doubt been smudged. He stood and stepped back to give her space, his expression indecipherable. Or she didn't have the mental capacity to figure it out and was too distraught to call upon her databases. She inhaled, swallowing as if she could ingest her alarm and thus pacify it, and smoothed out the navy pleats of her sailor's dress. She flashed him what was hopefully a reassuring smile. "I'm just a little tired. I didn't sleep well last night. But I'm glad you're back. Let's get you set up with a computer again."

Chapter Ten

E verett followed as Betty once again escorted him to the computers, like yesterday. But today was nothing like yesterday. She had been calm and in control then, gracious and welcoming. Now, she was a shell of that. Pretending to be calm and in control when she was anything but.

When he'd entered the library and she had not greeted him, he'd worried something had happened. Then he'd found her on the loveseat, every bit as delicate as a glass figurine. She was unharmed, as he'd first worried, but struggling to pull herself together. He watched as she worked through breathing exercises, her eyes closed and her body posture straight. But she wasn't calm or relaxed. Her breaths were uneven, her face contorted with passing emotions, and a soft whimper escaped each time she swallowed as if it pained her.

Everett had waited for her tense muscles to relax and the anguish to ease from her expression. After several deep breaths, she was no closer to composure. Quite the opposite, in fact. He had to do something to distract her from her rising anxiety. Hell, he'd stand on his head and juggle chainsaws and make fart jokes if that would help her.

Even now, he worried. She walked quickly, her strides too short as if her muscles were taut to their limit and about to snap. As if to relinquish the slightest bit of control would result in an utter breakdown.

And he had no idea how to help her. After his weird dream last night, he was similarly out of sorts and his steps, unstable like the floor beneath them, heaved and wobbled. They reached the computers and she turned to him, her hands clenched together at her waist, fingers entwined, her expression pinched.

She inhaled to speak, but he spoke first. "Betty, you didn't answer my questions. Which is ok... that's your choice. But please let me help you."

She sniffed and glanced at her blue heels with white trim that matched her sailor dress. Then she pasted on a smile and chuckled. Both were brittle and unconvincing. "I'm fine, Clark. Thank you for your concern. I'm sorry I didn't hear the bell chime when you walked in. And I'm sorry you had to witness me behaving in such an unprofessional manner."

He frowned at her words. "What do you mean, your *unprofessional manner?*"

"I mean curled up on a couch, weeping and wailing like Mrs. Bennet from *Pride and Prejudice.* It's hardly proper behavior." Betty chuckled again. It was every bit as forced as the first one. "What would the neighbors... uh..."

Her voice trailed off and her pupils dilated, her gaze drifting to over his shoulder even though there was nothing behind him she hadn't seen a thousand times. The false levity in her expression eased until her face was an emotionless mask, her eyes unfocused and her lips slightly parted as if she'd forgotten to close them after her last word left her tongue. He'd seen this before, but never on a human. She looked like an automech waiting with a machine's infinite patience for orders to be downloaded. A computer booted up and ready for software installation, its cursor blinking endlessly. This, on top of his assumption that her behavior was out of character, sent chills through his body. In a moment, she'd lost all animation in her lovely face, leaving it a blank canvas that was no longer Betty, but instead whatever someone else wanted her to be. And the words that had died on her lips… *What would the neighbors…* what? What would the neighbors think? It wasn't an uncommon expression, but something about it hit a deep memory. That phrase was meaningful somehow. Connected to something he should, but couldn't, recollect.

Several racing heartbeats had passed, and she had not moved.

"Betty! Snap out of it!" Everett's heart pummeled against his chest. This—whatever *this* was—was bad. It meant something, and his gut told him that meaning wasn't a good thing. It was scary. Scarier than three drunk attackers. Scarier than an attempt on his life.

The urge to run away jerked his muscles, but isn't that what he'd already done? He could only run so far and for so long. While his life might be more at risk if he turned to face danger, at least he might glimpse his adversary and face it like a man. Or better yet, face it like Betty, head held high and a ready quip on the tongue.

He reached out to shake her back to the moment, but she blinked and shook her head. Her face resumed its animation, and her look of confusion would have been adorable if his heart wasn't still racing. Her lips pursed. "I mean, what if Mr. Bingley arrived to court my dear Jane?"

She laughed at her attempted joke, but Everett could only frown. She'd continued the conversation as if she hadn't just spent a dozen seconds staring into a void. Did she not realize what had happened? How could he explain it to her and would she even believe him?

"Betty, you weren't doing anything unprofessional when I came in. Especially not considering what you've been through. I was merely worried. Did those three guys threaten you again? Do we need to call your officer friend again?"

Her brows furrowed in confusion and the effect was adorable. Before she could respond, he continued, keeping his voice low and soft as if coaxing a frightened bunny from its burrow. "Betty, I know why you sent me away yesterday, before your officer friend arrived, and I appreciate your concern for me. But... do *you* feel safe? Are you afraid those guys might attack again? Do you have backup if they do? God knows you were a badass yesterday, but please don't think you have to defend yourself alone. No one should have to handle their problems all by themselves. And no one should have to feel unsafe."

He grimaced at his words which contradicted his own life. He'd often felt unsafe and unable to handle his problems, but he'd never had anyone he could trust to help him. Well, at least not anyone who hadn't eventually left him when his problems got to be too much. In a perfect world, his words should ring true.

"I'm fine. Thank you for your concern, Clark." She frowned again.

Everett scrubbed at the whiskers on his jaw, not believing her claim. "Uh, if you say so. But please let me know if you have another brain fart. It was a little freaky."

Her eyes widened in surprise. "Brain fart? When did that happen?"

"Just now." He shrugged. "You spaced out and stopped talking for several seconds."

Her expression collapsed for a moment before she pulled herself together. She *humphed* in disdain and turned toward the front of the library. "I'll have you know ladies do not *fart*. We simply release wisdom from both ends."

Then she flashed him a saucy wink and tossed her curls over her shoulder before striding away.

Thank God the Betty he knew was back. Or at least some

semblance of her. Everett sank into the chair and rubbed his eyes. Between his bizarre nightmare-dream last night and the episode at the loveseat minutes ago, he wasn't sure he could handle much more. His world had turned topsy-turvy since he'd buckled himself into his plane less than a week ago. "What the hell just happened?"

It was a rhetorical question with no answer, so he settled in front of a computer and began the painful startup process. *What would the neighbors think?* The phrase which prompted Betty's robot-like response. Why was it so familiar? He stirred it around his brain, trying to grasp the trail which connected it to a memory while the computer slugged through its startup commands until he could sneak in for another—hopefully good news this time—foray into the back alleys of the internet. *What would the neighbors think...about Preditech's CEO sneaking around like a thief?* Well, Preditech's *former* CEO. Everett clenched his teeth at the reminder, and dug down into his search.

He hadn't gone far when the sound of Betty's footsteps approached. Odd that he could hear her. The floor was carpeted, and her steps should be silent. He chuckled as he switched the screen mode back to the *Trib's* front page. Knowing Betty the little bit he did, she made sure not to sneak up on anyone. A couple awkward confrontations with patrons using the computers to watch porn would teach such a lesson.

He turned as she stepped into the open space of the computer area, and caught his breath again, like he did each time he looked at her. She was truly a beautiful woman. Even with his life as fucked up and at risk as it was, he still appreciated the vision she made. Her gentle curves, the slope of her calf, the hint of cleavage, the sensuous sway of her hips, and the warmth of her smile. If she gave even a half-hearted attempt to seduce him, he'd be a goner.

Blood rushed to his cock at the thought, the traitorous appendage. Sex was the last thing he should be thinking about, but the damned thing acted like he was back in high school sitting next to one of the pretty cheerleaders. He was still a homeless man, though. Betty didn't not hold her nose and squeal in disgust around him. That didn't mean she wanted him.

"Clark, I grabbed you some clothes last night while I was shopping for Toddler Time supplies." Betty leaned her hip against the table and held out a heavy sack, much like she'd brandished the amenities bag yesterday. "I had to guess on your size. And they're not fancy."

"Betty, you're Santa Claus, the Easter Bunny, and the Tooth Fairy all rolled into one." He gripped the sack, never so grateful for something as previously trivial as clean clothes. It didn't matter if they were the size of a tent or made him look like a clown, he'd wear them like a trophy. Everett opened his mouth to thank her. "I can't pay you back for this."

What the fuck kind of thank-you was that?

The joy in Betty's eyes dimmed at his blurted words, and he cursed himself for being a thoughtless idiot. For being everything she wasn't. Before she could respond, he tried to recover. "I'm sorry. I mean, I know you would have led with that. I'm not… not used to freebies. Or handouts. I meant to thank you, but the wrong words popped out of my mouth. Your kindness and generosity have been, well, more than I've ever expected from anyone. Thank you."

She relaxed, and her smile returned. "I put a fresh amenities bag in the bathroom for you. I'll bring lunch in a couple hours."

"Betty, you're an angel." Everett stood to head to the bathroom. He couldn't get out of these disgusting clothes fast enough. As he passed by, he leaned down and planted a quick kiss on her cheek.

Holy shit! He jerked back. Why had he kissed her? His heart pounded in shock. He hadn't meant—

She turned to him, her eyes wide and her mouth open in shock. She touched a gloved hand to where he'd kissed her. God, he'd really fucked up now. He scrambled to apologize. "Betty, I'm so sorry, I—"

She smiled again, a soft blush shading her cheeks. "It's ok, don't worry. It's just been a long time since anyone has… thanked me… in that manner. Now, go on and do your thing and I'll get back to work."

Everett hastened away, afraid he might do something equally as impulsive. Like pull her into his arms for a real kiss. Once locked in the bathroom, he stripped and cleaned his body as effectively as possible with only a sink, a washcloth, and as much lather as he could produce from the small bar of soap. As he washed below the waist, thoughts of Betty sprung into his head. His other head sprang to attention and he bit his tongue to stem the moan that rose up. Betty wasn't the only one who hadn't been… *thanked*… in a long time. Everett gripped the edge of the counter with one hand and wrapped the soapy palm of the other around his erection. This wouldn't take long, especially as vivid fantasies of a certain sexy librarian flitted through his mind. There was no doubt a special kind of hell for sick bastards who masturbated in a library bathroom, but he could no more stop than he could have kept Antony from pile-driving his jet into the earth.

Several minutes later, he emerged, squeaky clean from his field bath, and luxuriating in fresh clothes. Yet still soiled deep in his soul.

Everett found Betty standing in a romance section, frowning at the slender, rectangular holo-book in her hands. She hadn't heard him approach again, lost in her own thoughts. A troubling picture because she seemed like she would be always aware of her surroundings. Today's Betty was such a stark contrast to the Betty he'd met yesterday. She shoved the book back into the rack, muttering to herself. "Nope. Can't stomach a *secret baby* today."

In the silence of the library, he heard her softly-spoken

words. Her muttering continued, increasing in frustration as her fingers skimmed the multitude of offerings. "No *accidental pregnancy. Surprise baby.* Not even an *M-preg.*" Her gaze swept the books before she plucked a book out with a brooding sigh. "Looks like it's going to be a *bad boy billionaire.*"

Was there a special meaning behind her selection? He cleared his throat. "Bad boy billionaire?"

She turned on a soft cry, her eyes wide with surprise. Had she forgotten she wasn't alone? Which also seemed oddly uncharacteristic. Everett gripped the amenities and bag of dirty clothes so he didn't do something stupid. Something stupid such as pull her into his arms and kiss her. As if any woman who had been threatened with rape not twenty-four hours earlier would have sexy thoughts on her mind and the desire to pursue them with a homeless man, even if he was bathed and wearing clean second-hand clothes. He mentally kicked himself for the unbidden desire to taste her lips.

Betty sucked in a breath, blinking and shaking off whatever fear had drawn the color from her face. She composed herself again, cloaked in her librarian's mantle.

"Yes. *Bad boy billionaire.*" Her voice wavered with emotion. So, not quite composed as she no doubt wanted to appear.

She cleared her throat and looked at the book in her hands, her meticulous brows pulling together in concentration as she continued with a surer tone, like reciting words she'd said a thousand times. "It's a popular romance trope, much like its historical counterpart, the reformed rake. Of course, by today's standards, it's more accurate to say *bad boy trillionaire,* but that doesn't flow off the tongue as nicely. The basic premise is usually a powerful, self-made CEO with a fleet of private jets and a harem of gorgeous socialites at his beck and call, yet he falls for the spirited small-town girl because she's the only one who sees through his tough exterior to the secret past he's hiding and still love him. And"—she waved a hand—"other variations on that theme."

Everett's heart lurched and his cheeks heated. Was Betty talking in general, or did she know about him? He scratched the thickening stubble on his cheek to hide his reaction. "I suppose the billionaire is also devastatingly handsome and an amazing lover."

A hesitant smile lifted the corners of her lips. "Oh, you know the trope?"

"Know it? *Pfsh...* I've lived it." He shrugged dismissively. Betty huffed a laugh at what she no doubt assumed was a joke, not realizing how close to the truth she'd hit. Except, well, the *harem* was a bit of an exaggeration. And even *bad boys* likely had higher standards than to jack off in library bathrooms. And there was no one—small-town or otherwise—to whom he dared reveal his secrets. "So, bad boy and billionaire... Is that what women want in a man?"

"What women want from a man...?" Her face screwed up in a frown as she considered her answer. She glanced around the aisle and clasped the book against her chest. "You shouldn't take romance books as a literal guide. There's too much diversity in the genre to land on much commonality for that. And there's a lot to be said for the sheer escapism involved in reading any manner of fiction. However, I think romance gives women permission to embrace their own polarizing desires."

"Desires? I assume you're not talking about what they want in bed." *Please talk about what you want in bed.*

He leaned a shoulder against the bookshelf and tucked his hands into the pockets of his new jeans, which happened to fit him perfectly, to keep from reaching out. A red curl had escaped and dangled at her temple like a siren's call, luring him against the rocky shores of his own surging desire. Desire which shouldn't exist because he'd just taken care of the matter, dammit. But something about the quiet intimacy of standing so close to Betty, drowning in the soft soprano of her voice, lost on the lulling waves of her lips. How he managed to string a complete sentence together was a miracle.

"Physical desires are one aspect of romance." Her teeth tugged on her bottom lip, and Everett swallowed against the swell of desire, wishing those were his teeth nibbling her plump pout. Her hand lifted to the side of her neck as she worried her cherry lips and stared into a distant memory. Everett nearly moaned as her fingers trailed her slender neck from ears to collarbone, the very same path he wanted to take with his tongue. If her actions had been at all calculated, he could have walked away without the slightest roll over in his pants. However, her absentminded caresses were about to undo him. He struggled to keep aware of their conversation.

When Betty continued, her words were hesitant and measured as if pulled from a deep, unfamiliar well. "But romance is about so much more than sex. They're about the personal growth of the female protagonist. They're about a healthy romantic relationship. I think many women like the idea of having a man who shares the daily burden of life, even when she is perfectly capable of taking care of herself. That a man loves us *for* our imperfections, and not *in spite of* them. And maybe we learn to do the same. That a man cherishes our love and offer up his own without using any of it as leverage or defiling it with selfishness. That love is not restricted by trivial things such as money, geography, social status, or physical attributes. That, for each us, there is at least one person who finds us beautiful, desirable, and—above all—worthy."

She stared at the floor and tapped her fingers against the holo-book in her hand, her voice soft, wistful. "At least… that's my theory."

Her explanation nettled in his gut, like a muted alarm, a warning her words were a challenge. A challenge he would fail because he couldn't offer any of that to a woman. Up until five days ago, he could offer money, social status, superficial companionship, and—let's be honest—decent sex. Now, he could only offer paranoid companionship and decent sex. As if any worthy woman would want that.

More blaring than the alarm her words triggered, was the sensation something still had Betty out of sorts. Gone was her ready wit and her calm, unflappable confidence. She hadn't called him out on his deflection with a simple smirk or lifted eyebrow. She hadn't countered his bullshit with her own good-natured style. What had happened to pull the cover off her vulnerability and expose it like a gaping wound? He had his own Pandora's Box of problems to deal with, so it would be crazy to even contemplate taking on whatever burden she carried. But it was there: the desire to slay dragons for her. A truly odd sensation, because he wasn't the slaying knight. He was the evil dragon.

An evil dragon that couldn't tear his eyes from the silky curl on her forehead. He gave into the temptation. Slowly enough so she could stop him—hell, slowly enough so she could have him hog-tied on the ground—he reached out and brushed the curl back. She held her breath, held still as his fingertips traced from her ear, down her cheek, and along her jaw to her chin.

"That's…" He cleared his throat. "That seems like a pretty tall order for a book." Everett dropped his hand to his side before he did something even more rash, such as back her up against the bookshelf, cup the back of her head, and kiss her thoroughly.

Betty sighed long and low. Perhaps as disappointed as he? "Yes, well, a romance book *is* fiction. But maybe that's why the genre is so popular. Because those authors overcome the impossible by bringing the readers exactly what they want and expect."

"I see. I'm more of a *Chicago Trib* guy, myself." Everett offered as an apology.

Betty's smile was a tad too bright and brittle to be sincere.

She was no doubt trying to cover up whatever she was dealing with. "Yes. And you still have research to do, right? I'll be at the front until it's time to spill some lunch for you. Otherwise, I won't bother you."

She winked and stepped to his side as if to pass him in the narrow aisle, but he stopped her with a palm up. "Betty, you're not a bother. You're a godsend." He nodded toward the bags still in his hand. "Thank you for the clothes. With everything you have going on, you shouldn't have felt like you had to get them for me. But I appreciate that you did."

"Clark, it wasn't much. I'm glad the clothes fit." She waved away his gentle chiding. "And I'm not sure what you mean by *everything going on.* Other than today's Toddler Time program, my days are pretty boring."

He frowned and stepped closer. "You consider three men attacking you *boring?*"

She blinked, as if she'd forgotten yesterday's tussle. Everett ground his molars in exasperation. So much for walking away from Betty's problems in lieu of his own. "Dammit. Three men assaulted you, Betty. Or at least tried to. Does that sort of thing happen so often you don't think anything of it?"

One hand on her hip, she struck a seductive pose and pretended to flip a lock of hair over her shoulder. "Well, it doesn't happen as often as it used to."

She was deflecting his concern. He recognized his own tactic. He nearly called her out on it, but the shimmer of regret in her eyes stopped him. This topic obviously made her uncomfortable. He was an ass for pushing. "I'm sorry. I don't mean to make you relive what happened. I'm just grateful your self-defense skills saved us both."

Her eyes flicked to the side and her head dipped in the barest nod. She was hiding something. Whatever secret she had, he needed to leave it alone unless he wanted to spill his own. He needed to respect her privacy because he wanted the same in return. Even though every cell in his body clamored to know her more intimately, to know her secret so he could help keep her safe from it. As if he still had that kind of power and influence. As if he'd ever had more than a veneer of that kind of power and influence. Real power and influence didn't leave a man destitute and alone in a strange town with no one to turn to and someone trying to kill him.

Everett had better keep that reminder top of mind, and keep the temptation that was Betty at arms-length.

Instead, he leaned in and brushed his lips against hers in a gentle kiss. *Fuck, he was an ass!* Before he could pull back and apologize for his ill-timed and uninvited sexual advance, she placed a warm hand on his chest, her fingers gripping the shirt fabric. His pulse raced. She didn't shove him away. In fact, she tugged him closer and sighed softly against his mouth. He might be a selfish bastard who had nothing substantial to offer a beautiful woman, but he wasn't stupid enough to pull away.

So he slanted his head and kissed her like he'd wanted to since he'd first walked into the library. Kissed her like he needed her oxygen. She followed his lead with her own passion, fanning the flame of his desire until his cock throbbed as if he hadn't recently spanked his monkey. He pulled her against his chest, one hand against her shoulder blades and the other tracing the curve of her spine. She moaned, her lips parting, and he slid his tongue inside, exploring the warm recessed of her mouth, memorizing her sweet flavor. He couldn't get enough of her.

Lost in the wonder of her kisses, Everett had no idea how long they stood there in each other's arms, their lips dancing. Betty pulled back after what seemed like an eternity—but still wasn't long enough for him—and he cursed the breath of air which now separated them.

"I'm sorry." *Ugh.* There he was, blurting more ridiculous words. "I mean… I'm not *sorry*, sorry… That was amazing and anytime you want to kiss me, I'm one hundred percent on board.

But I acknowledge my advances might not be welcome and my timing wasn't the best. Not after everything you've been through. I should have asked your permission. I should have... I should have been a better man... I shouldn't..."

He was blabbering, and she looked disappointed. She placed two fingers against his lips to stop his verbal spewing and he dropped his arms to his side. "No need to apologize, Ev-um, Clark. I appreciate your concern, but I'm okay. I'll let you get to your research."

She turned and walked away like she hadn't just rocked his world. Such an easy dismissal, when he'd been aroused and conflicted and concerned. Like yesterday, she'd taken control of the situation and he was left with nothing to do but go along with it. He almost laughed at his own transition from bad boy billionaire to needy homeless boy toy. Did Betty have any romance novels with that kind of hero?

No. Who would want to read that?

Chapter Eleven

Betty held herself together until she sat down at her desk. Once there, she covered her mouth to stifle her moan and crossed her legs against the throbbing need between them. Sweet baby Jesus, Everett had looked sexy in the simple t-shirt and jeans she'd bought him at the thrift store. The clothes clung on him like a gold-digger socialite, accentuating his muscles and his lean build. The aubergine-colored shirt made the dark gray of his eyes pop, and the faded jeans… they hugged all the right spots.

And he'd kissed her. His lips had worked a magic on hers that she'd only ever known in romance novels. Her uterus had convulsed and heat had erupted between her thighs as if he'd kissed her there instead. She'd nearly forgotten her body was capable of arousal, much less such potent desire. Then again, she hadn't been kissed or caressed in such a long time, it was little wonder her body so wildly reacted to his impulsive smooch.

Insta-lust romance, aisle three.

In her wildest dreams, she never would have thought she'd share passionate kisses with Everett Dean. Or any powerful CEO, for that matter. She struggled to calm her body's reaction to it. In spite of their impromptu make-out session, he wasn't here to flirt or play around with her. He probably didn't even have sex on his mind, and she should be more concerned his presence would bring unwanted attention to her cyborg status. Even so, her body yearned for more of what that kiss had promised. When he'd been covered in layers of dirt and sweat, she could view him as someone in need of help, charity. She could keep him at arms-length and not get her emotions—or her sexual needs—involved.

Something had happened between the moment he'd first walked into the library and a few minutes ago. Something to turn her interest from philanthropic to physical. Was she so horny she'd jump the first decent man who walked in the library? If that was the case, she would have had sex with Grady a long time ago. She would have welcomed the gang bang yesterday and thanked Paul the Asshole and his pals for their time. Those thoughts shot stomach acid up her throat.

Maybe Everett had programmed all his systems to trick cyborgs into lusting after him. That might explain her powerful response to him. The thought stopped her cold. She laughed at her own wild imagination. Why would Everett Dean want an army of cyborgs—male and female—turned on by his mere presence? What a useless thing to have, and he didn't strike her as the kind of person who put up with uselessness.

"Get your head out of the bedroom, girl." She muttered to herself. "Maybe you need a break from reading romance for a while. It's got you all worked up and not thinking straight."

This wasn't a work-related issue. She couldn't paste on her librarian's smile and make it all better with a book recommendation. She couldn't quip her way to back to familiar territory. For whatever reason, even after such a tiny bit of time in Everett's company, he was more than merely fascinating, more than any romance trope she'd read. More than *alpha hero*. More than a *bad boy billionaire*. More than *nice guy next door*. Hell, even more than merely *forced proximity*.

This was real life, and she shared her library with a man who so much more than any romance characters. He was the hero, the villain, and the victim. Was this was even supposed to be a romance? Maybe it was political thriller.

Maybe it was horror.

Whatever it was, she needed to stop lusting after Everett. Needed to help him… but help him with what? Get back on his feet so he could continue running Preditech and creating cyborgs the world hated? Figure out who was trying to kill him, and likely get herself killed in the process? Assume a whole new identity and begin a new life somewhere far from here, so she'd never talk to him again?

She rested her head on the cool surface of her desk. The good news was her overthinking had evaporated her arousal for the time being. The bad news was now she had a massive headache.

For the second time today, she sat and inhaled calming Pranayama breaths, but with slightly better results. So focused on easing the pounding in her head, she nearly screamed when the front door swung open. When Charlie entered, she nearly screamed again. His visits were always rare and never on consecutive days. Yet he'd been here yesterday, asking her to meet with Eve Myer. Eve, who had been a Preditech executive. Who had supposedly died in an apartment fire, like her boss had supposedly died in a plane crash. And yet, both were still very much alive. Alive, and in Betty's life.

Fuck her life. And fuck the Pranayama breathing exercises. She was going to start drinking.

"Charlie, what a surprise." Her voice quavered from the riot of emotions she battled. Hopefully he didn't notice, although his wary nature likely caught even the slightest change. "You never visit two days in a row. What brings you here? Can I finally talk you into sharing lunch with me?"

His gaze scanned the rows and aisles as was his habit. He shook his head. "No thank you, Miss B. I'm honestly only here to encourage you to reconsider yesterday's invitation. I think you'd be interested in what the lady has to say."

Fear fisted her gut and froze her blood. She struggled to breathe. "What does she have to say that would be so interesting?"

He shrugged, seemingly oblivious to her stiff, clipped words and the fact she hadn't smiled yet and was probably as pale as death. "Not exactly sure what she's going to say."

"Not even a broad idea? A general topic? Are we talking politics, knitting patterns, crisis-management techniques, Cephalopod reproduction?"

Charlie shrugged his shoulders. He knew. He *had* to know. Otherwise he was some mindless lackey doing another person's bidding, and she would never label him as such. He was street smart enough to survive and avoid getting in trouble with the authorities. Intelligence glinted in his eyes, giving the impression his homeless situation was a choice rather than an unfortunate series of events, unlike what Everett had experienced. So, if Charlie chose this life, there must be a reason for it.

Like the fact there must be a reason why he again urged her to meet with Eve. And the secrecy of it all hit a raw nerve.

She marched up and stood toe-to-toe with Charlie, crossing her arms and spearing him with a glare. "Charlie, you know more than you're letting on, and it's annoying. The *she* we're discussing is Eve Myer. Why does she want to meet with me? If you won't answer that, then I'll decline the invitation and ask you to leave me alone."

Charlie's eyes rounded in surprise at her harsh tone. He glanced down and shuffled his feet. "Um, I mean no offense. I'm just passing along the information."

"Passing along information that has taken you across the city from the Park 100 camp, on foot, twice in as many days. Yes, I know your home base is there, so don't play naïve with me. Come clean. Why is it so crucial I meet with Eve?"

He hesitated for several long moments, seeming uncomfortable with sharing whatever information he had. After clearing his throat, he looked at her, his eyes pleading. "Miss B, you won't be disappointed if you meet with her. And that's all I'm comfortable saying. Please trust me on this?"

"That sounds like something a serial killer says to lure his victim into an unmarked van. Trust you? Our relationship is not strong enough for me to blindly trust you or Eve Myer. I can't accept this meeting."

She dropped her arms on a thought and lowered her voice in concern. "What does she have on you? Are you in trouble? Is she blackmailing you? Threatening you?"

Charlie flinched back a step, his arms raised to ward her off like she was an evil spirit, and his brows furrowed at her questions. But he didn't look frightened, only surprised. She'd never pushed him like this, and the result was awkward for both. But Betty didn't let up. "Charlie, I can help you if you need it. I have a detective friend I can call."

He shook his head so his tangled mass of hair beat against his shoulders, his hands held up to ward off her intensity. "No, no, it's nothing like that. It's just—" His gaze caught something behind her and his body language instantly morphed, folding in on itself again, shoulders hunched and head lowered submissively. Here was proof Charlie's usual demeanor was merely an act. Why would a young man like Charlie choose to be homeless?

She glanced where he stared at Everett, who stood at the end of an aisle, fists clenched as if ready for battle but his expression blanched, like he'd seen a ghost.

"I-I'm sorry Miss B. I thought you were alone." Charlie beat a hasty retreat toward the door. "I'll leave you—"

"Charlie, you haven't answered my questions—"

He called over his shoulder as the door closed behind him. "Please reconsider. I'll be back."

She hastened after him, but he was already gone. No retreating figure on the sidewalk, no shadow rounding a corner, no evidence he'd been there. Had she imagined it? Betty closed the door and glanced at Everett, who hadn't moved but looked confused and perhaps a tad bit terrified. Everett, who was Eve Myer's boss. Both of whom were supposed to be dead, but neither were.

She whirled on him, her emotions running high and needing an outlet. "What are you doing here?"

"I heard raised voices and thought it might be those guys from yesterday." He recoiled from the shockwave of her harsh tone and held his palms up as if to ward off a physical attack. "I'm sorry, I didn't mean to interrupt your conversation."

Like yesterday, he'd come to her defense. If she weren't so overwrought, she might be flattered. Instead, her alarm stepped up a notch. Of course he came to her aid; he was using her and needed her alive.

He swallowed hard, his Adam's apple bobbing. "Wh-who were you two talking about?"

Snap! There went her patience. She shook a finger in his face and hissed. "You know good and well who we were talking about. Just like I know good and well who you really are. Everett Dean. Preditech CEO. A man who is supposed to be dead, but you happen to be alive and here in my library. And your former executive Eve Myer, who is also supposed to be dead, is alive somewhere in this city and wants to meet with me. Why? Why are you here? Why here of all places? What do you want from me?!"

She advanced like an angry tiger, and he retreated with each step until his back pressed against the unforgiving side of a bookshelf. His expression grew more panicked with each word from her mouth. Like he'd seen a ghost. Like Betty was the specter of Death calling him to the Underworld. If she kept pushing, his heart might stop, and then she'd have an actual dead body to deal with and questions from the authorities she'd have to answer.

She stopped her advance and her barrage of questions. He stared at her, his chest heaving and his eyes wild with fear. She'd called his bluff, and he hadn't responded like a man in control of his destiny. He was cornered prey. She ran his reaction through her body language database. It had been originally installed so she could determine a target's level of interest, but she didn't use it these days. Too much of a reminder of what she truly was. However here and now, she needed every advantage with Everett to figure out his motives.

The result came back positive: He was scared. She nearly rolled her eyes. Thank you cybernetic enhancements for detailed information no normal human could possibly figure out themselves. *Ugh.* Some secret spy she was. Little wonder her assignments had been so bottom-of-the-barrel. Betty sighed, all fight and flight drained from her limbs. She rubbed her temple to ward off the returning headache.

"S-someone tried to kill me." Everett blurted, still circling in the tailspin of panic she'd shoved him into. "My pilot knew something was up and saved me. But now, the DCO is taking my company. I'm supposed to be dead, so they'll take my years of hard work and intellectual property like it's theirs and everyone is thrilled with it but me and I can't stop them or else they'll learn I'm still alive and try to kill me again."

She canted her head to the side, trying to keep up with his rushed explanation. He was telling the truth, at least his truth. As he spoke, his voice rose in tenor, his eyes darting around the room as if expecting assassins to strike. Then he frowned. Calm determination washed over him—she sensed it more than she could see its effect, but he stood taller, more controlled than he had been moments before. He looked at her and she saw the resolve in his gaze, felt his determination in her bones.

"I came to your library because someone here hacked into

Preditech's network, and it was my only lead to get my life back." His voice resonated with strength, such a change from a moment ago when she'd feared she'd broken him. He reached out and stroked her cheek with the backs of his knuckles, the barest of touches as if he worried it might frighten her. His volume dipped, softened. "Then I met you. And your kindness has given me hope. Hope to start fresh. Because I don't think I'm ever getting my old life back."

An emotion she didn't dare use her programming to translate sparkled in his eyes, and his lips curved upward. His gaze lowered to her lips, and she wrapped her hand around his. Need blossomed again in her belly, which triggered warning bells in her head. Yes, she wanted him. But her history of getting what she wanted had proven to be rare and a double-edged sword. She worried she'd end up run through the gut this time. For a few turbulent heartbeats, she waffled between leaning in for the kiss he promised and running the other way.

Caution won out.

She cleared her throat and pulled away. "Everett, if you don't mind, I have some work to do before I dish up lunch. But please let me know if you need anything."

Her typical customer service words sounded hollow to her own ears. But she didn't care. She scurried to her desk and, after several moments, Everett walked back to the computer area, leaving the library once again quiet as a church.

No, wrong image. Quiet as a coffin.

Betty rubbed her temples, closing her eyes and willing back the tears that burned at the seam of her eyelids. She shouldn't have outed Everett on his duplicity. She'd known his secret; she didn't need him to admit it out loud. She shouldn't have said those things to Charlie. She should trust him and agree to meet with Eve, if only to learn what the woman wanted from her. She didn't really know Charlie or Eve, but her gut told her they were intrinsically good people. That, while they had secrets, those secrets weren't meant to hurt *her.* At least not intentionally. But years of trusting the wrong people and the wrong promises made her wary. She couldn't trust her gut. It had steered her wrong more times than not. Which meant, even if Eve and Charlie did not intend to hurt her or put her in harm's way, accepting the invitation to meet would still put her there.

With so many odd coincidences and unanswered questions dropping unannounced into her life, her self-preservation kicked in. She wanted to jump out of her skin. She wanted to pace. To move. To run. Run. She should run. Run out, pack her things, skip town, run away. Better to start again than risk the little life she'd built for herself here. Than risk her life. She'd find a small town out west, create another new identity, start fresh where no one knew her and no one would find her.

Her age must be catching up with her because the thought was exhausting. She was tired of running. She wasn't a spring chicken anymore, and running away once again was like… being chicken. She could stand up against three brawny men without batting an eyelash, but an unknown ramification from the presence of a certain library patron had her jumping out of her skin and near tears.

Some badass spy she was.

She sat at her computer and inhaled yet more calming Pranayama breaths, again with poor results. Her body was too tense, her heart too troubled, to calm down. This morning, she'd told the Toddler Time moms knowledge combatted ignorance and misconception. Maybe it could help overcome her irrational fear and the screaming desire to flee. She settled more comfortably in her chair and removed the glove on her left hand. Her fingertip datajack would hasten any internet searches she needed to accomplish.

It was time to arm herself with everything she could learn about Everett Dean, Preditech, and Eve Myer.

Chapter Twelve

Everett's heart rested firmly in his throat, beating at the pace of a stampede, as his fingers flew across the keyboard. He'd marched to the front of the library when he'd heard Betty raise her voice, prepared for round two with the three guys and pissed they'd had the audacity to return at all, much less so soon. But all fight had whooshed from his bones the moment Betty had said that name.

Eve Myer.

Then, she'd said that other name. Everett Dean.

Betty knew who he was. Had figured it out, because she was smart like that, and he'd been an idiot for thinking he could waltz around without being recognized. The real question was how did a librarian in an Indiana suburb three hours from Chicago by way of the HyperBus know his former exec? And why were Betty and a homeless man talking about meeting Eve? Meet with Eve, who was supposed to be dead, burned to unrecognizable ashes in an apartment fire a week ago. A day after downloading the mysterious virus from his private company network.

Not unlike his own story: supposedly dead, burned to

unrecognizable ashes in a plane crash a few days ago. After discovering someone had planted a mysterious virus onto his private company network. This strange coincidence had all the markings of more *wacky shit* to fuel his recently acquired paranoia.

Had Eve planted the virus? Planned the apartment fire? Hacked his pilot? Granted, she'd only been with Preditech for about a year, but he'd never once thought the soft-spoke, bean-counting divorcee was capable of such espionage. However, recent events had him questioning many previous assumptions. Everett had walked halfway across Indiana to get to this library because it was the source of the mysterious IP address that had pinged Preditech's network security. Had he walked into a haven or a trap? The questions further fueled his flight instinct, the impulse to run knocking at his nerve endings. His sense of urgency laser-pointed, lending speed and focus to his efforts as he dove deeper into the corners of the internet. Battered by questions. Searching for answers. Infiltrating.

But he could only do so much from this antique computer, and the forced limit scraped against him like sandpaper. Everett clenched his fists against his thighs, frustration grappling with helplessness. Hiding in a library, waiting for the world to be set to rights so he could return home—as if that was even a possibility anymore—clawed against his need for action. For solutions. But what could he do? He was one man with no resources. Brazen attitude alone wouldn't fix anything or secure his safety. And honestly, he didn't have much brazen attitude at his disposal at the moment. A near-death experience and being homeless knocked that out of a man. What he did have in spades was petty retribution, which offered an outlet for his need to do something, even if that something solved nothing.

If he couldn't fight his enemy face-to-face, he could at least pester the hell out of him.

Everett hacked the national banking system so ATMs across

the country would randomly spit out cash siphoned from the Preditech accounts. He reprogrammed the employee break room TVs in Hawks's department to only show porn channels. And he rerouted the Preditech senior management phone extensions to the Vietnamese restaurant three streets over from the office.

He hadn't solved anything, and he'd fallen back on his old hacking prank days. But it would lead Preditech and the DCO on a merry chase trying to find the source of it all. And it was wrapped in the pretense of being proactive. At least, it wasn't wallowing in self-pity. It certainly removed a smidgeon of doom and gloom off his shoulders.

He chuckled a soft yet evil-villain *mwa-ha-ha* in the quiet of the library. "My, my... what would the neighbors think?"

His fingers paused on the keys. Again, that phrase rang with familiarity. Something deep in a core memory... or something more recent maybe... the connection was elusive, almost aggressively so. Like his brain was saying *forget this memory,* the insistence of which triggered his newfound suspicious nature.

He muttered the words out loud again, quietly into his fingertips. And that same sensation in his brain rolled down to his belly. *This is important* his gut told him while his brain continued the mantra *This is not the memory you're looking for.* The contradiction itself was proof enough. This phrase was meaningful. But for the life of him, he couldn't figure why.

Well damn. Add it to the steaming pile of helplessness and unanswered questions he stood knee-deep in.

"I hope you're hungry, Everett." Betty called out, always giving him enough time to switch screens so the *Trib* popped up and hid what he was really doing. When she appeared, her expression was as flat and tired as her voice.

He'd never seen her so out of sorts as when talking with the homeless guy—Charlie, she'd called him—earlier in the entryway. Her posture had been tense, agitated. She'd raised her voice and gotten up in Charlie's face, and then had gotten up in

Everett's face. He wasn't an expert on her moods and mannerisms, but she clearly hadn't been happy to see Charlie. In fact, she'd reacted like a cornered wild animal, hackles raised, claws out, wanting to flee but forced to fight instead. Even three burly attackers hadn't brought her to such a level of agitation; she'd been composed and had dominated the situation. Yet this one homeless man had stripped away all manner of control with his invitation.

She had acted the way Everett felt. Scared. Distrustful. Afraid for his life. Carrying an enormous secret that could ruin him if anyone found out. A secret that wasn't exactly a secret anymore, since Betty knew who he really was.

She kept her cards close to her chest. She clothed herself in outfits which gave the impression of innocence, reminiscent of a more simplistic era. She didn't share any personal information, instead hiding behind a demeanor of friendly customer service no one bothered to question. Even when he'd found her, trembling and agitated on the couch this morning, she had swiftly cloaked her vulnerability with professional restraint and deflected his concerns. Her speech about romance novels had sounded the most personal, but it still offered no details to her life. What did he know, he was only a man... but her words seemed like the wishful thinking of any woman who had lived to a certain age.

He couldn't expect Betty to share the intimate details of her life after such a short period of time, and not to him, a stranger, and a homeless man. He'd suspected they had something vital in common: secrets. Well, at least until she'd figured out his secret. Still, she guarded one or more of her own, with a skill and grace he wished he had. He was more than a little curious what a beautiful, poised woman such as Betty had to hide with such care?

Oh, yeah. She had some whopper secrets.

"Betty, I'm always hungry." He answered her as she set a

plate piled high with baked chicken, pasta salad, and watermelon slices on the table beside the keyboard. There was enough for three meals. He glanced up at her, a quip about feeding an army dying on his lips when he noticed the fragile smile she offered him. "This looks delicious. Thank you. And thank you for not—"

What, exactly, was he thanking her for? For not freaking out that he was Everett Dean? For not calling the authorities on him? For not kicking him to the curb the moment she'd figured it out?

She waited, her head cocked to the side and an eyebrow raised as if she expected him to lie. Again. He hadn't outright lied to her. Just hadn't told her the truth. Well, he'd lied about his name. And mislead her. And hidden what he was doing on her computers.

He sighed and scrubbed the back of his neck, his shoulders drooping beneath the harsh truth of his deceit. "I'm sorry. I'm sorry if I've done anything that will hurt you or put your livelihood in jeopardy. By being here, I've put you at risk. And I wish I could take it back. I wish I could undo what I've done. I was so desperate for help. For answers. For a reason *why*. I'm just… I'm sorry, Betty."

Was Betty even her real name? Probably not. After Everett had moved out of his dad's house, he'd changed his name, taking his deceased mother's maiden surname as a total *Fuck You* to his rigid, emotionally unyielding father. Fortunately, his father had passed away long before Hawks had sidled up to Everett. And Hawks had been so hungry for Everett's cybernetic genius, he'd had the government approval paperwork pushed through, ensuring no scandalous or questionable background information was unearthed. Can't have the world's largest government arm-in-arm with someone who'd spent time in juvie. *What would the neighbors think?*

Hmmm… that phrase still niggled at his gray matter.

She nodded as if she'd made a decision and cleared her

throat. "I have a lot to think about, Everett. Enjoy your lunch and let me know when you're finished. I made chocolate chip cookies last night."

Then she left.

Everett chowed down on his meal like it was his last one. Which it very well could be. Nothing was assured these days, not like they had been even a week ago when he'd known exactly what to expect from his employees, the DCO, and himself. Now, the only certainty in his life was the uncertainty.

His searches yielded nothing unusual, if one considered the information from Everett's newfound perspective: there was no deed so dastardly it would surprise him. So, he wasn't surprised to learn his jet crash had been deemed pilot error, a complete loss with no survivors, and no need to spend resources on pursue further. Neither was he upset to read a corporate communication to his employees from Richard Hawks, stating the new focus of Preditech's systems would be strictly militaristic. Oddly enough, he wasn't even stunned to learn a few former girlfriends gobbled up the social spotlight with tear-stained declarations of having loved him, and if only he hadn't been so emotionally wounded and distant, maybe they still could have stayed together, blah, blah, blah.

And the media gobbled it all up like it was a pan of Betty's brownies. He was the main topic of all the news, from business to celebrity, from hard-hitting to tabloid. They dissected every aspect of his life, from his work to his lovers and finally to his untimely death. Whether they idolized or demonized him—and most of them demonized him—everyone was talking about him. As if he was the most important person in the world.

Joke was on them. His life was going to straight hell. Hurtling earthward to explode into a flaming pile of debris, much like his plane and pilot. And Everett couldn't figure out a way to save, stall, or avoid the resulting crash, much less piece any of his life back together. So much for the brilliant mind that had figured how to fuse cybernetic systems with the cells of living organisms. Currently, his brain couldn't figure its way out of a paper bag. Even with hours of mindless work at his fingertips, with nothing to contemplate but how to wrest Preditech back from Hawks and the DCO, and stay alive while doing it, he drew blanks. Not a single idea or even a glimmer of a general direction in which to head. Nothing. Nada. Zilch.

He was well and truly fucked.

"Are you ready for cookies?" Betty's voice came from the small kitchenette on the other side of the library. Gone was its flat tone; she sounded more like the Betty he'd first known, although still subdued. She must have taken this time to work through whatever had her so out of sorts earlier. Or she'd strapped her acting prowess more tightly around herself. Whatever the case, though he hoped it was the former, the gentle timbre of her voice reminded him of childhood summers and birdsong. A more artless, halcyon time of life, untouched by ugliness and greed. The perfect childhood as only advertising agents and the entertainment industry could envision it. The *Leave It to Beaver* days that never actually existed for anyone, but which everyone sighed and reminisced about as if they had. An innocent era one could practically taste—hot dogs and corn-on-the-cob and lemonade and Fourth of July parades—even if one's own childhood was marred by abuse and neglect. The unsullied dream of innocence. Of possibility.

Betty's voice was as pure as apple pie and baseball games, and modest as a school marm... on a woman who was his most sensual fantasy come to life. Whose body was an invitation to sin. Whose eyes gazed at the world through the lens of experience. Whose words were filled with battles fought, some lost, but most won.

If she could overcome whatever challenges she'd experienced, he could do the same. Watching her stand toe-to-toe with her adversaries lent him strength and the determination to face his own. He might not have immediate answers or battle plans, but that didn't mean he was giving up.

Perhaps in the meantime, he could be useful to Betty.

She slid a plate piled with thick homemade chocolate chip cookies and a cold glass of milk on the table. Everett stared at the feast. More cozy images of hearth and home that he'd never experienced wafted through his head as the warm chocolate aroma filled his nose. His belly was already filled with chicken and watermelon, but he'd be damned if he'd decline these luscious treats. Surely there was room for at least one. Maybe two.

She leaned on the table, her voice laced with understanding. "If you're too full, don't force yourself. Take them with you instead."

She didn't seem ready to address the elephant in the room—his duplicity—and he was grateful for the opportunity to stall that inevitable discussion. "I'm too full to eat all of these. But if I take them with me, I'll share them with my homeless neighbors. I used yesterday's brownie as currency to get a shady spot under a tree for the night."

"How positively entrepreneurial." She chuckled. "Do you need more?"

He laughed at the idea. "I could find a happy mouth for any brownies and cookies you want to provide, but don't feel you have to bake just for me to give it away."

She sat a hip on the table to face him. "Baking is easy enough. And if it would bring joy to those down by the river, I'd be more than happy to provide you with them."

Everett leaned toward her. Their camaraderie was stilted, but she seemed to want to try to move past the awkward phase, which was a relief. The thought of having to walk away from her —or of her walking away from him—had physically hurt. "Betty, I can be your errand boy and deliver desserts to that population. But you should be the one to get the accolades and appreciation for your hard work, not me. Yes, I'm down and out, and your handouts are most welcome. As are the amenities and the clothes. But I'm not a freeloader."

She popped to a stand as if he'd reprimanded her for some offense. "I didn't mean to make you think you were, or that I thought of you in that way—"

"That's not what I'm saying. Betty, you've been perfect. I want you to know I'm not expecting anything. That I'm used to paying my own way. No, I don't have money to give you. But I can work. I don't have any skills, but I'm fairly strong."

"What do you mean, you don't have skills?" She stared at him as if he spoke a foreign language. Then shook the expression away. "Perhaps, you mean like, you'd be willing to do some menial work around the library? Like cleaning or weeding?"

Her words were hesitant, as if she expected him to sneer at the possibility of a little manual labor. God knows he'd done worse in his life. Getting dirt under his nails might be one of the most honest day's work he'd ever accepted. He held his hands up, previously manicured and callous-free palms out, and wiggled his fingers. "These are yours to work to the bone."

Chapter Thirteen

Betty left Everett to enjoy his cookies and continue his internet search. Not because she had any pressing responsibilities or he'd specifically requested privacy, but because she sensed a change in their dynamic. He didn't seem to consider her merely as a means to an end. He... he *saw* her. And that was unnerving.

She didn't consider him as a drifter in need of a friendly handout. Neither did she see him as merely Everett Dean, CEO of Preditech. He was something in between. Something different. Something interesting. And she couldn't seem to walk away from that. She'd brought him the amenities bag to spend time with him. She'd bought him new clothes because he'd desperately needed them. But mostly to see if they would look as good on him in real life as they had in her imagination. Her imagination had failed miserably.

Her libido didn't seem to mind.

And when Everett had waggled his fingers and offered her their use... well, the first few duties that had popped into her head hadn't been cleaning or weeding.

What was wrong with her? Preditech's supposedly dead CEO

was hacking into secret government sites via her library computers, certain to be discovered and result in a very public raid by a heavily armed SWAT team. Both Betty's and Everett's futures, their lives, the fact he was still alive, and her cybernetic status would be exposed. They were doomed.

And all she could think about was kissing Everett Dean.

There had to be an explanation for why her body and head were at such odds today. Her CPU must be overheating. Some wiring somewhere had loosened. One of her systems was malfunctioning. Hell, maybe she was going through The Change. Did cyborgs even go through perimenopause? Her cyborg conversion had included a hysterectomy, which might have prompted an earlier start to that biological process. But where were the hot flashes? And the mood swings, or the vaginal dryness, because honestly, there was nothing dry down there, especially since Everett had walked into her life. Her cybernetic systems had been designed to keep her hormones at natural, healthy levels. She should be functioning like normal.

But there was nothing normal about how much she wanted Everett. The need grew with each hour and those thoughts had shoved out everything else. Including basic self-preservation, apparently.

"Miz Betty, is everything okay?"

Grady's voice sounded in the entryway, and Betty turned with a yelp. She'd been so caught up with her inner conflict she hadn't heard the bell chime. Everett's presence had her off her game. Grady was the last person she wanted to see, but on the upside, his intrusion was more effective than an ice bath.

"Good afternoon, Detective Grady." She cleared her throat and struggled to sound as professional as ever. Even to her own ears, her tone was flat and her words clipped. "I didn't expect to see you again so soon. What brings you here again?"

"Now, Miz Betty, don't be cross with me." Grady placated, his annoying twang a little too southern for this part of Indiana.

"I came to see how you were faring and if those boisterous boys had returned or otherwise been in contact with you. Just looking out for your safety 's all."

"Well, as you can see, I'm fine. And those three *grown male assailants* haven't been back. Thank you for your concern. Enjoy the rest of your day." She was through being nice. After their conversation yesterday, she was in no mood to be pandered to, so cared not a bit she sounded bitchy.

"Excuse me, ma'am. I've reshelved all the books you gave me." Everett's calm voice, making up some silly task she'd never given him, washed over her nerves like a balm. She turned to him, shocked he'd expose himself so readily to an officer of the law. What if Grady recognized him? Everett stood at the opening of an aisle, looking at her, his expression concerned. "Do you have any more books for me to put away?"

"Oh, I thought you'd be alone." Grady sounded perturbed to discover she wasn't. "So, I see you're, uh… You have a work exchange program for the homeless now? Something to help them pay for library services?"

Betty clenched her teeth against the biting retort that popped into her mouth. Instead, she kept her attention on Everett, noting the spark of irritation in his gaze as he slanted a surreptitious glance at Grady. Seemed he didn't like Grady's attitude either. Betty smiled and spread her hands in apology. "No, unfortunately I don't have any more books, Clark. But the plants need watered, if you don't mind. The watering can is under the kitchen sink. Thank you for your help."

He returned her smile. And if she wasn't imagining things, he also winked at her before ducking his head and assuming a semblance of the stooped posture Charlie always affected. "Happy to be of service, ma'am."

He retreated toward the kitchen and tension filled the pregnant pause. When she turned back to Grady and spoke, it was slowly, as if explaining a simple concept to a simpler individual. "Detective, a work exchange program would be superfluous. All library services are free and open to the public. There is no direct cost to work off."

"Library services aren't *free.*" The detective countered in a voice that managed to sound more patronizing than before. "They're paid for with taxpayer money. Homeless don't pay taxes."

"Your services are also paid for with taxpayer money, and law enforcement never refuses an emergency call to the homeless camps." Betty leaned her weight on a hip to appear calm and casual, when she was anything but. Didn't Grady realize every word spewing from his mouth pushed her further away? Any attraction she might possibly have felt had been long ago turned to ash and blown away.

"The police take an oath of office." Grady shrugged, dismissing her argument with a grunt and a jangle of pocket change.

The man was utterly obtuse, and she was ready to drop kick him into next week.

"I also take an oath, Detective. And I will not discriminate against those who don't pay taxes such as children and the homeless. *Especially* children and the homeless who need our services more than any."

"I see I've made you mad, but I—"

"Very observant of you. Now that you have officially checked on me and found me unharmed, you may go about your day. Thank you."

"Miz Betty, I think you misunderstood my words. I'm trying—"

"I'm a librarian, Detective Grady. Words are my work, and their proper usage is a powerful tool in effective communication. I assure you, I did not misunderstand the words you spoke. Perhaps *you* made a poor choice of what words came out of your mouth."

"I'm just concerned for your safety, that's all." His southern twang got heavier as her steely tone continued to ice over.

If this conversation lasted much longer, Grady might call her *darlin'* or tell her she'd be a lot prettier if she'd smile, and forensics would have to mop his remains off the library walls. "We had the conversation about my safety yesterday, detective. And my opinion on the matter hasn't changed. Good day."

"You were attacked, and now you're all alone—"

"Not at all alone—"

—"with a strange man who has who-knows-what-all intentions toward you—"

"His intentions are to provide menial services in exchange for the lunch I shared with him. I understand it's contrary to your professional experience, but not everyone is a criminal."

"Your naiveté is going to get you in trouble one of these days, and then you'll be calling me again."

"As I am a tax-paying citizen and you have taken an oath, that shouldn't be an issue."

"I'm trying to prevent that situation from happening."

"Prevention by taking away my freedom of choice is tyranny."

"Ooooh, I think you're overreacting a bit there, darlin'."

The air fairly crackled as Betty tensed. A loud cough nearby ripped her attention away from Grady and her desire to dismember him. Everett stood at a plant stand several feet away, watering can in hand, coughing and shaking his head. "I'm so sorry, ma'am. I just choked a little. Please forgive the interruption."

His coughing fit distracted her from the verbal and physical flaying she had prepared for Grady. Everett made sure to keep his face averted from the detective. She reached out to him. "Clark, there's lemonade in the refrigerator. Please help yourself to a glass. It might help calm your throat."

The detective fairly growled. "Can't you see Miz Betty and I are having a conversation?"

"No, we're not, Detective Grady. We're having a fruitless argument. We need to agree to disagree, and go our separate ways. I thank you for your swift response the other day, and your conscientious follow-up today. I give you permission to consider this case closed and move on to more pressing matters."

Detective Grady rocked back on his heels and rubbed his shiny pate, his face and bald head the dull red of frustration. Betty almost pitied the poor guy. He probably didn't even know why or where his misguided good intentions had jumped the rails and crashed into her determined self-sufficiency.

"I actually came here on official business, Miz Betty." He shuffled his feet a moment, then spared a meaningful glance toward where Everett had walked. "If you have a moment, I'd like to talk to you."

Betty followed the direction of his gaze, and shrugged. "We could have been doing that all along, but you chose to lecture me instead." Normally, she might back down and don her customer service mantle, pretending she wasn't insulted. Today, she couldn't muster the energy.

The detective rocked back on his heels and jangled the change in his pocket, obviously uncomfortable. "I'm… concerned for your well-being, Betty." Gone was the affected twang. "I, uh, recently learned I didn't support a former partner as much as I should have. It's a regret that hangs heavy, you know. I don't want a repeat of that. Especially not with a woman I'd hoped would see me as more than just a detective."

"I appreciate your concern. *Detective*." Betty hugged her torso, her voice soft with regret. Not because she regretted anything she'd said, but because she couldn't bring herself to regret not returning his interest.

Grady gaped at her for several heartbeats, as if waiting for a confession which never came. After a few moments of tense silence, he sighed in resignation and pulled out a notepad from his shirt pocket. "We've received an anonymous tip that someone might be using the library services to defraud government agencies."

Betty's heart jumped to her throat, but her cybernetic systems worked to filter that shot of adrenaline. As a spy, she couldn't show emotions or physical reactions, or at least, that had been the explanation she'd received about this special system. Her heartbeat remained calm, but the worry remained. Had someone already noticed Everett's internet searches? Had he already been tracked here through the city's street security cameras? Was the SWAT team already on its way?

She cleared her throat. "That's a pretty sweeping accusation considering the broad reach of government and its agencies, one of which is the library system itself." Betty forced her voice to sound calm. Bored, even. "Unless your informant gave you more details, it's likely you've been pranked."

"They said that person might be utilizing the library computers to access restricted information." Grady made it sound like that was the ultimate clue in a political mystery the proportion of the Kennedy assassination. His even preened like a strutting rooster.

Betty wasn't about to take the bait. "Well, assuming you're talking this particular library and its specific patrons, we had Toddler Time this morning. I'm pretty certain the Broad Ripple mothers and their children were here to enjoy reading and some craft activities. However, a few children staged a bit of a mutiny when they decided they were cyborg dinosaurs. I could list their names if you wish. And if you have a warrant."

Grady's triumphant grin dimmed slightly.

"We also had a poetry reading about a month ago." Betty continued, dropping her arms to her side so she didn't appear defensive. Although her tone was light, every word she uttered dripped with *go fuck yourself.* "One of the attendees was highly displeased with the event, although you're already aware of this because he and his friends are the ones you spoke to yesterday. I'll defer to your expertise whether he was merely drunk or trying to defraud the government by attacking me. Now, we do have a healthy online service for our videos and digital books. I've noticed an increased trend in teen patrons checking out retro manga movies, if you feel that should be further scrutinized."

His face was flushed with either embarrassment or anger. "What about other patrons?"

She shrugged and lifted her hands in supplication. "What other patrons, Detective? I've had fewer than I can count on my fingers, and those are long-time residents. However, bring me a warrant and I will be happy to give you their information."

"I mean, you know—" Grady canted his head toward the kitchen area. They both turned in that direction, to find Everett pausing mid-stride, two glasses of lemonade in his hands, like he'd been caught in a criminal act. Grady glared at Everett and continued. "The vagrants who you welcome in. It's unseemly for you to be here alone with their kind. What would the neighbors think?"

Her mind blanked. Her vision narrowed on Grady like he was at the end of a dark, blurred tunnel. His voice muted as if heard through a wall or a body of water. Her body tensed, readying for some yet-unnamed action. Time slowed. Seconds glittered in the air as if the laws of gravity and motion no longer applied. The blood in her veins paused its passage and the air in her lungs hung, unused. Anticipation ballooned in her head, waiting. Waiting for…

Waiting for what?

"Betty?" Grady' concerned voice broke through her expectant haze. She blinked, her mind and body back in the moment like nothing weird had occurred a moment ago. "Betty are you okay?"

"Sorry, what were you saying?" She blinked. What the heck

had just happened? Why had her body reacted in such a weird manner?

Grady huffed in irritation. "I'm saying there's no good reason for the homeless to use the library."

Betty glared at the detective, indignation at his prattle and concern for her body's unusual response rising like a molten tide. "Just because the homeless lack a permanent residence, does not mean they are uneducated or stupid. They simply lack the ability and funds to secure entertainment that you and I take for granted, and the library offers this to them for free. The local newspaper, reading materials, movies, etc. Computers give them access to employment sites. The books offer them self-guided educational opportunities. Everything they need to better their life. But you seem to think they don't deserve any this."

President Kennedy's Cuban Missile Crisis couldn't have been this tense. She and Grady stared at each other for several moments, waiting for the other to speak. Preferably words of apology.

Neither did.

Grady finally coughed and rubbed his head. "I'll... I'll take my leave, then, Miz Betty. But please don't hesitate to call if you need me. That offer stands."

Neither Betty nor Everett moved as the detective turned and walked out the door. Neither spoke until the muffled sound of another door closing and a car driving away reached them. Betty released the breath she'd held and turned to Everett, who handed her a glass of lemonade.

She took a small sip, wishing it had gin in it, and offered him a tired smile. "I'm sorry you had to witness that."

His gaze was still locked on the front door, his lips pressed in a thin line, the jaw muscle at his temple twitching. He looked at her, his gray eyes stormy with emotion. "I'm sorry your detective friend is a dick."

Chapter Fourteen

"You stare at your drink any harder, and the glass is going to break."

Everett chuckled as his voice pulled Betty from her morose contemplation. She gasped like she'd forgotten where she was or the fact he sat next to her, so caught up was she in her own thoughts. Or maybe because his voice had practically boomed in the silence of the library.

After her run-in with Grady, she'd wanted something packing more punch than the glass of lemonade he'd offered. He was happy to oblige, having discovered a dusty bottle of gin in the cabinets while searching for glassware. Given Betty's excited reaction when he'd retrieved it, she probably had never noticed it.

They whipped up a pitcher of London Lemonade and she'd led him to a small couch in a cozy corner offering a contented oasis for their private little Happy Hour. She sat so close he could smell the subtle scent of rosewater and verbena on her skin, mixing with the juniper and lemon of the cocktails. He inhaled, trying not to sound like a snuffling bloodhound, and let the aroma fill his senses. The early evening sunlight filtered in through the leaves of the outside trees and reflected off the colorful mosaic artwork displayed on the vertical surfaces of shelf and wall space, bathing them in a gentle kaleidoscope of colors. If only he could piece together the broken chunks of his life and create a misfit design equally as pleasant.

His cynicism laughed at the wish. That wasn't his life anymore. Truth be told, that hadn't ever been his life. His life had never been contented or tranquil.

Driven. Turbulent. Fierce. Unforgiving. Those were the words to describe his former life.

And he wanted to return to that?

Everett swirled the yellow liquid in his glass, the ice cubes tinkling like merry bells. He swigged his drink, enjoying its lively herbal tartness. If he drank enough, maybe he could drown out the truth. His cynicism laughed again. He'd become a bumbling drunk if he tried. And he wouldn't get to fully enjoy the company of the strong yet delicate woman seated next to him.

His ice clinked in his empty glass. He'd sucked his cocktail down so quickly condensation hadn't had a chance to gather. Betty quirked an eyebrow at his empty glass and he shrugged. "What can I say? I'm a gin man, and that was a tasty beverage."

She reached for the pitcher to offer him a refill, but he lifted his hand to stop her. "And it goes down way too easy. You'll get me drunk at this rate, which I wouldn't mind if your intent was to have your wanton way with me."

Her shoulders jerked and a sound emerged from her mouth that was a rather unladylike snort. Rather than take offense, his smile broadened. "In that case, I'd better slow down on the alcohol."

She shook her head and offered a weary apology. "Sorry, I… haven't had much luck with drunk men recently."

That wasn't a memory he wanted her to associate with him.

He smiled and swirled the ice in his glass, glancing sideways at her. "Ah, the it's-not-you-it's-me rejection."

Before she could offer another lame apology, he speared her with a sincere glance. "Betty, it's okay. I've received harsher rejections from women who aren't half as nice—or enticing—as you."

She dropped her gaze and stared into her drink again. Everett almost laughed. He'd never had to work this hard for a woman's attention. He'd never had to carry the weight of the conversation. And for the first time in his life, he wanted plenty of both from the woman sitting beside him, her shoulders hunched and her thoughts obviously troubled. Turns out, he wasn't skilled at any of this. If only she were a cyborg, they'd at least have something in common they could discuss.

"So, what made you realize I'm Everett Dean?" Crap, he hadn't meant to blurt that. "I mean, I supposedly died in a plane crash. Why would you think a homeless man could be me?"

She gawked at him like he had a few screws loose, and answered with caution. "I can't imagine how you survived that crash, and I didn't immediately know it was you. But after you washed up, there was no question. You look like him with a five-day growth of facial hair."

He shrugged. "So I have a beard and dark blond hair—"

"No. You look *exactly* like him, down to your height, weight, age, build, and mannerisms." She continued, ticking off a finger with each fact. "Your clothes and bag are designer brands. And fresh off this year's runway, so they would not have made it all the way down to the give-to-the-homeless pile yet. You don't *act* like a man who's been homeless for any length of time. You showed up at my door four days after the crash, which is how long it would have taken a person to walk from the crash site to here."

"Those are some nice coincidences. But not proof." He was

playing devil's advocate here, and she had ready answers that shredded his rebuttals.

"And, aside from your pretense of reading the *Trib*, your internet history has revolved around Everett Dean's personal accounts, Preditech's corporate network, and the DCO."

She threw out her final bit of evidence like a poker player laying down a royal flush. His cheeks heated. It might be an educated guess based on the assumption he was Everett Dean, but there's no way she could know for certain where he'd been. He'd scrubbed his tracks too well for anyone to trace. "How do you know what my internet history has been?"

She sipped again, then cupped her hands around her glass. "I'm a librarian, Everett. I offer patrons access to information as well as books and open mic poetry readings."

"Do you make a habit of scrutinizing what your patrons do on the computers?"

She frowned as she nodded. "Yes, I do. Before I got this job, the library was embroiled in a child sex-trafficking ring coordinated through its community computers. And on occasion, a patron will think our computer area is a safe place to view porn. So, I've been forced to become nosy, and I won't apologize for it."

"It's one thing to be nosy. It's something else to track internet footprints which have been scrubbed."

"I'm pretty fluent in reading all those digital zeros and ones. Especially finding those that people try to hide." Leaning back, she pinned him with a hitched eyebrow. "You're either the world's best impersonator, or you're the actual Everett Dean. And my money is on the latter."

He tried to call her bluff. "If you're so sure I'm Everett Dean, what else do you know about me?"

"You mean, beyond what's found on Preditech's website, your Wikipedia page, and the thousands of news articles about you?" She raised an eyebrow over the rim of her glass as she drank. He didn't have to answer. "In the wake of your supposed death, the DCO has snatched up your company with some bogus eminent domain excuse, and your employees are happy to let this happen because they never liked you anyway."

Ouch. He hadn't expected her to be so blunt, even though it was the truth.

She continued. "And that PR nightmare news leak about Preditech ignoring the fatal flaw in their implant systems has been silenced with suspicious swiftness now that you're supposedly dead. Almost as if it had been planted for the sole purpose of getting you on a plane to D.C."

He blinked, a strangled chuckle bubbling up his throat. "Damn, you're more paranoid than I am."

"Yeah, well, I've been at it longer." She muttered into her glass.

"So why does Eve Myer want to meet up with you?"

She tensed, her exhale a disgruntled huff. "I don't know why she wants to meet with me. Charlie won't or can't say, and short of meeting with Eve, I can't fathom why she would be so dogged in her invitation. She came here asking to use the computers, like you. She lasted a couple hours before she raced out the door without another word to me. She'd sent an email to a local reporter and then found her own profile on social media, which is probably where she learned she was supposed to be dead."

He scrubbed his beard, sighing. Her information corroborated his own. There was something to be said for having someone he could share his predicament with. Maybe he wasn't entirely alone in all this. "Your library is the IP address that pinged Preditech's network the day after Eve's brownstone burned down. Without a better place to start searching for who'd want to kill me, I came here."

"Do you think she faked her own death?"

He shrugged. "I'm not sure, but I don't think so. She copied a virus someone planted on my personal company directory. That virus is what started the media frenzy about Preditech's negligence. Eve might be a whiz with numbers, but not the digital kind you're apparently so well-versed in."

Betty toyed with a pleat in her skirt, yet still offered no apology for snooping on his internet searches. Not that he expected or wanted it. In fact, he liked that about her. Her tenacity. Her refusal to back down. She'd stood up to three aggressive drunks, one sexist police detective, and a deceptive homeless man.

God she was an angel. And too good for him, even if he could have his old life back. Especially if he could have his old life back. The Everett Dean from even a week ago was an asshole, and not deserving of a woman as beautiful as Betty. Hell, the current Everett Dean was probably still an asshole and still didn't deserve her. Never would, no matter what he did. Gramps had told him the right to be with a good woman had to be earned, every day. Everett hadn't earned his time with Betty, not even close. Even so, he desperately wanted to kiss her again. Wanted that connection to something good in this world, as if it might wash away his sins. He wanted to cup her cheeks and taste those intoxicating ruby lips, like wine at a dying man's last meal. Without conscious thought, his body leaned toward her and his hands lifted to cup her cheek, but he caught himself.

Angels didn't kiss devils like him.

Everett's shoulders dropped and he stared into his glass as if the ice cubes were divination tea leaves he could interpret. A weary sigh left his lips. "You ever dream of running away and starting fresh someplace?"

The question blurted before he could bite his tongue. Betty's low chuckle shocked him so his gaze cut to her. Her smile held a mischievous glint, but there was a hint of sadness in her eyes. "Dreamed it? I've lived it."

Everett couldn't help the small smile as she lobbed his own

words from earlier back at him. Had she known there was some truth to his statement? Was there some truth to hers?

"Everett, I would never judge someone's decision to stay with or run away from the life they have. There's a whole community of people over that knoll by the White River who have made the same choice." Betty lowered her volume to nearly a whisper. "In fact, most of us are tempted, or forced, to make that choice at least once in our lives."

He fiddled with the seam of his jeans. "Look, you're right about who I am. But you're also smart enough to know it puts you in danger. Having me around puts you in danger. I don't want you to get hurt. But I also have no idea what to do or where else to go."

Her hand rested on his forearm. "Your secret is safe with me. I know that's an empty promise right now, but give me a chance to prove it." She set her empty glass on the side table and faced him. "We'll work together to form a plan to help you either recapture your previous life, or find a way to begin a new one."

He glanced around the serene room as evening darkened around them, the scene at odds with the riot of thoughts and feelings coursing through him. How he wanted to take her up on her offer. He certainly couldn't solve anything alone, a fact he could finally admit. But he also wanted her to be safe. And helping him was a surefire way to be the opposite of safe. He should walk away from Betty and leave her to her life. But she was his only hope.

He shouldn't admit that to her, even if she'd already figured it out herself. "Why are you so eager to help me?"

She inhaled deeply and met his gaze. "Throughout history, there have been people used as scapegoats for another's ignorance and fear. Those of the Jewish faith. Salem's witches. America's indigenous tribes. The homeless. That abuse always reflects poorly on the abuser in the light of hindsight, not that it helps the abused while it's happening. I believe cybernetic individuals are the target of today's societal woes, and I'd like to, in my own little way, minimize the damage our history books will one day show for it."

"Meaning, you're a cyborg sympathizer." His forced the disdain in his voice. He obviously didn't feel that way, but it was the most common assumption where his life's work was concerned. Anyone at all pleased with—or even ambivalent toward—cybernetics was an object to ridicule. Or worse.

"I'm an advocate for understanding and empathy." Her spine straightened and her shoulders pulled back, as if daring him to call her that again. "Attacking or demeaning those who are different makes no one happier or more content with their own life."

"Spoken like a cyborg sympathizer."

She bristled at his obtuseness and glared at him. He couldn't hold his humor in any longer; he laughed, his shoulders shaking at how delightful she was to tease.

She shot him a dark scowl, then swatted his shoulder good-naturedly before chuckling. "And you're the biggest sympathizer of all."

He winked at her, then shook his glass so the ice cubes clinked. "Well, see here now, Miz Betty." He affected Grady's awful southern twang. "If we're going to solve the worlds woes, we're gonna need more gin."

Chapter Fifteen

Betty paced her tiny living room, her hearing tuned to the sounds of Everett showering in her bathroom. With each anxious about-face as she reached the edge of her area rug, the hem of her skirt swished and threatened to catch on the bric-a-brac decorating her coffee table and display shelves. If she didn't calm down, something was going to break. A knick-knack, her composure, or both.

Her apartment was small, and she'd worked hard over the years to make it a welcoming home with her eclectic tastes. But she'd never before invited anyone in, so couldn't have anticipated how tiny it would feel with the addition of a second person. Granted, that person was physically bigger than she was. And just… larger. An important person. In spite of the fact he was trying to hide, Everett Dean was a major personality. A celebrity. He came with an enormous reputation, a large ego even if it was currently dented, and the weight of society's opinions and expectations.

With all that, there was barely room left in her apartment for her raging desire. Oxygen had to be shoe-horned into her lungs.

Her thoughts were reduced to what he was doing right now, naked, lathered with her soap, water sluicing down his—

"Pull yourself together!" She hissed, plopping into a chair and burying her face into her hands.

If she'd known her hormones were going to detonate like this, she wouldn't have suggested they come here for a private, after-library-hours planning session. Should have let him return to the homeless camp for the evening. Should have walked home alone and maybe taken care of her own needs quickly and quietly, then gone to sleep without stressing about what to do with Everett Dean. But Grady's tip worried her. Someone knew about Everett's internet searches, even if they didn't know who had conducted them. The library would be under digital scrutiny and likely physical surveillance as well. Someone was bound to figure out what was going on, and by whom. It was only a matter of time. They needed a plan to implement, and soon.

"What am I going to do about Everett Dean?" She whispered into her hands. She'd promised to help him, promised they would figure a plan together. But intent was the only thing she had to offer. She had no plans, no suggestions, no ideas. Only a growing desire for him. As if that would keep either of them safe.

But what would?

"My days of being the *strong female character* trope were a few years ago. Am I even up to the task?" She lifted her head and drew in a deep breath as the water in the shower turned off. Then, she stood and straightened her skirt with a resigned sigh. Her badass spy days might be a distant and not entirely pleasant memory, but she'd survived this long on sheer will, determination, and some well-timed quips. She could manage a bigger challenge just fine. A smile toyed at the corner of her lips. "Besides, why should the young have all the fun?"

She walked to the kitchen to check on the pizza in the oven, listening to the soft pad of Everett's footsteps out of the bathroom, through the living room, until they stopped at the kitchen entrance. "Dinner is almost ready." She called over her shoulder as she closed the oven door and placed the mitts on the counter. "Are you okay with Chianti, or do you want another gin cocktail?"

She turned to him, and her jaw dropped. The chenille robe she'd lent him to wear while his clothes were in the wash was wrapped sideways around his narrow hips, falling at angles and edges down his long legs like a trendy skirt. It's fluffy texture and carnation pink color, a few shades darker than his skin which he'd scrubbed to a bright glow, should have offered a comedic picture. Instead, it heightened her awareness of his masculinity by leaving so much of his svelte body uncovered. His torso was bare, a smattering of light brown hair on his chest and trailing down from his belly button, his chest and abs fit from regular exercise without being bulky, his arms strong enough to catch her should she faint. Should she faint and test them? He was a feast for her eyes more decadent than any chocolate dessert. More savory than the pizza in the oven. She was never going to wash the robe again.

Dinner is served.

"Oh, it is?" Everett glanced around. "It smells delicious."

Dear lord, she'd said that out loud. She clamped a hand on her mouth to stifle the yelp and whirled away, frantic to find the wine and get busy with something that didn't involve drooling over Everett's nearly naked body.

Large hands covered hers as she grabbed the bottle. His voice, deep and rich, rumbled in her hair and tickled her ear, and the heat of his body warmed her backside. And other places. "Betty, let me open that, please. You've done all the work so far and I don't want to be useless."

She was the one who was useless. *All the work so far* had been to unwrap the frozen pizza and put it in the oven. But her mouth couldn't form coherent words to explain this, so she gave up and simply handed him the opener, then set the table. Her antique mid-twentieth century dinette with chrome trim and aqua boomerang-pattern Formica top complemented the turquoise restaurant-style vinyl bench booth set against the wall. She would have to sit next to Everett because there were no other chairs. His bare chest would be eye level for the duration of their meal and her thigh would brush against his every time either of them moved or turned to talk to the other. It would be the single most awkwardly aware and sexually frustrated meal of her life. Maybe they could skip directly to dessert. There was a tub of chocolate gelato in the freezer, although she had something more creamy-smooth and decadent in mind. Actually, if they did it right, it wouldn't be smooth; it would be wild and wanton and—

What if he didn't want her that way?

Her desire dropped to her stomach like lead. What if she was alone in wanting to be sexually intimate? Yes, he'd flirted with her. Yes, he'd even kissed her. But that wasn't proof he wished for more, especially with her. Given the beautiful, lithe socialites he'd dangled on his arms over the years, chances were slim he wanted a curvy, quarrelsome librarian. And she wouldn't blame him.

A silent, bitter laugh escaped her lips. "Ah, the it's-not-you-it's-me rejection," she murmured to herself.

"What was that?" His voice was again in her ear, but on the other side this time, as he leaned past her and placed two glasses of red wine on the table next to the plates. "You seem out of sorts, Betty. Is there something I can do? Something you want to talk about?"

He turned her to face him, but she only saw his puckered nipples and entertained a distracted thought about the apartment temperature. "Are you cold?"

He canted his head to the side at her random question. Then he glanced down at where her gaze focused, and he crossed his arms as if to cover himself. She tried to look anywhere but at his chest, and only succeeded in looking down at his groin area. His hands dropped to the robe material at his waist and fussed with it.

"I"—he coughed and tried again—"I'll cover up more if it makes you uncomfortable."

Her gaze shot to his. His brows knit with concern, and his voice filled with guilt. What kind of ogre was she to make him self-conscious about his body and state of undress? She had given him the robe, knowing it wouldn't fit well, if at all, but it was all she had to offer. She reached out and gripped his hands, stilling their nervous adjusting of the robe, then squeezed to reassure him and shook her head.

"You're fine, and I'm being rude." Boy, was that an understatement. "I'm sorry... I don't get many visitors and I've forgotten how to be a gracious hostess."

"That's not true." Turning his hands so his fingers threaded with hers, he huffed a laugh. "Look, I'm sorry for being awkward. I'm ... better at discussing organic-cybernetic interfacing than I am with... with this." He wiggled a finger between their bodies, indicating the two of them, but not specifying what he actually meant. Did he mean conversation? Flirtation? Sex?

The oven timer dinged, snapping her attention back to the meal at hand. Deciphering vague hand motions would have to wait.

Betty served the pizza, then slid in next to Everett, and they ate in awkward silence. Or, at least, she did. She concentrated on her savory slice of pepperoni, feeding the only hunger she was certain she could satisfy tonight, while averting her eyes from the boring spot where the robe-skirt parted on his thigh. The dusting of curly hair on his legs didn't entice her. Neither did the muscle which flexed, and she definitely wasn't curious how it would feel beneath her palm. Even more uninteresting was the bulge nudging aside the knot in the center. She wasn't staring at it, but did it just surge and lift?

She swept up her wine glass and gulped her Chianti, although it didn't assuage her thirst one bit. Then watched Everett eat his pizza, the motions mesmerizing and more erotic than she could have guessed. The way his jaw muscles tightened and released in a steady rhythm. The flick of his tongue as it swiped sauce from his lips. His throat constricting as he swallowed. The effortless way he did everything, not knowing how much she wanted to touch him, lick him… taste him. She swigged more liquid courage, even though she would never experience its benefit, and set her empty glass on the table.

With a quick glance at it, Everett reached over with the bottle and refilled it. Betty tried to laugh, but hiccupped instead. She shook her head, throwing his words from earlier that evening back at him. "You'll get me drunk at this rate."

Cyborgs didn't get drunk. Their cybernetic system filtered alcohol to avoid it. Something about it reacting with the soldered points on a motherboard. But she suspected that was an excuse and the real reason stemmed more from a need to control cyborgs. Couldn't have people with superhuman limbs getting drunk and starting bar fights. Or abusing their spouses and children. Or rampaging through rush hour traffic.

Or sleeping with a man who was certain to break her heart.

Everett Dean wasn't going to stick around; he was the type of man who loved and left. Still, she didn't stop the bold invitation which popped out of her mouth. "I wouldn't mind you getting me drunk, if your intent was to have your wanton way with me."

His gaze pierced hers as if seeing into her soul. A slow, rakish smile spread across his lips and a delicious shiver traipsed along her nerve endings. "Betty, I very much want to have my wanton way with you." He picked her glass and set it on the other side of the table, out of arm's reach. Then he placed his own next to it. "So no more wine for either of us."

He cupped her cheek and his head dipped until she smelled the faint hint of chai latte spice from the soap she'd given him. His warm breath brushed her face and his lips hovered millimeters from hers. "I don't want there to be any question we both want this."

His words trilled down her spine as he finally kissed her. His lips danced against hers, pulling her breath away and returning it with soft sighs. Their tongues tangoed—*sliiiide, sliiiide, flickflick*—until the inferno he'd stoked in her mouth reached her core. Betty moaned and clutched at his shoulders, arching against him, urging him with her body to pick up the pace. He merely pulled her so she straddled his lap and chuckled before continuing the steady onslaught on her mouth.

"Don't be in such a hurry, beautiful. I've wanted to do this to you since—" he pulled back, blinking in surprise. Then he shook his head and his lips tilted in a lopsided grin. "Well, since yesterday. But it seems like a lifetime ago."

He nuzzled her ear and neck as his fingertips traced from her jaw to her collarbone and along the dipping bodice of her dress. Then his lips followed the same path, kissing, nibbling, and licking. She ran her gloved hands over his exposed skin, thrilling at the firm, flexing muscles beneath her palms, raking her nails until his hair stood on end and he sucked in a soft groan. His erection pressed against her core and she instinctively rocked her hips, moaning at the sweet friction. Then he tugged down her back zipper and pulled her sleeves down her shoulders, capturing her arms against her sides and exposing her navy lace bra.

After several heartbeats of gazing at her breasts like he'd seen the face of god, he reached around her back to unhook the bra. He kissed her again, deep and demanding until he stole her breath and her chest heaved. Then he pulled back and slid her straps down her arms until the material rolled over the full mass of her breasts and was free of their weight. He watched the dramatic unveiling with the fascination of someone being given the secrets of the universe.

"Betty, you're so beautiful. Poets should write sonnets about you." His voice was thick with wonder.

The derisive snort escaped before she could stop it. Her defenses melted in the heat of his expression. "I'm sure your Chicago socialites would disagree."

He snorted this time. "What the fuck do they know."

Then he palmed each breast, plumping and squeezing, rolling her pearled nipples between his fingers. Leaning forward, he kissed them, laving them with his tongue, teasing them with his teeth until she quivered with need, moaning and sighing from the sensual assault.

She wriggled her arms out of their sleeve restraints, tossed aside the bra, and speared her fingers through his hair to keep him in place, not that he seemed inclined to leave. She kneaded the muscles of his shoulders and back, and continued the rhythmic grinding of her hips. Moaning each time his erection bumped her sensitized clit through the layers of clothes.

His hands left her breasts to delve under her skirt and clutched at her thighs and buttocks. When his fingers tangled in her undergarments, he pulled back in surprise. A quick flick at the hem of her skirt, and his eyebrows shot toward his hairline. He'd discovered her matching navy lace garter set.

By his expression, it was the best gift ever.

Everett swallowed hard. "I want to make love to you wearing nothing but this." He hooked the tip of a finger along the edge of a stocking then around the one of the garters and snapped it against her thigh. Betty swallowed her moan. His finger continued along the edges of her undergarments, stopping at her panties and going straight to where her arousal had soaked the fabric. He circled his finger over the moist material, then up to her swollen bud, pressing and strumming it until Betty squirmed in his arms.

He wasn't doing anything she hadn't done to herself a thousand times. Yet, for whatever reason she couldn't be bothered to contemplate right now, this was sooo much better.

Please don't stop.

He stopped.

Before she could growl her frustration, he kissed her again and explained. "You're going to finish too soon, beautiful. Bear with me a few more minutes because we've barely begun."

Bringing his finger to his mouth and sucking at her flavor left there, he planted a soft kiss on her lips, then he lifted her in his arms and padded to the bedroom. Moonlight filtered through her sheer curtains and bathed the dark room in streaks of soft illumination. He laid her gently in the middle of her bed's white comforter, and divested her of her dress and shoes. Then he one-handed the knot of his robe and it fell to the floor.

He stood at the foot of the bed, one knee braced on the mattress and his erection jutting proudly, and simply gazed at her with that same expression of awe on his face.

The intensity of it all was too much and she squirmed. She didn't deserve to be regarded with such veneration. She wasn't a good person. Good people didn't do the things she'd done. They didn't pretend to be something they weren't. They didn't lie.

He crawled up the bed until he hovered above her, so close his body heat was a sauna to her skin. Once again, the intensity of his gaze speared her so she couldn't look away. His pupils were wide and dark, the thin ring of gray around them like a lunar eclipse.

"Betty, if I do anything—*anything*—that you don't like or makes you uncomfortable, tell me. And if there's anything you want me to do, tell me."

Sweet baby Jesus, no one had ever said those words to her before. She swallowed the sudden lump away and draped her arms around his neck. "What if it's something I want to do to you?"

His head fell to her chest and his laugh emerged strangled. "Just, please have mercy on a poor man. I'm not sure how much I can take." Then he settled on his side next her and pulled her into his arms. "And I haven't even had dessert yet."

Everett kissed her as he reached down and slid a finger past the hem of her panties, spreading her juices and pulling more moans from her as he continued where he'd left off at the dinner table, circling and pinching her clit with aching slowness. The hunger in Everett's eyes and his magic of his fingers detonated her own need almost immediately. She clawed his broad shoulders and turned her head into his neck to moan her release.

"That was," she managed between panting breaths, "A very nice dessert."

His laughter rumbled through her body. He planted a loud peck on her lips and affected Grady's horrible twang. "Darlin' that was just getting dessert warmed up."

"No." She shook her head, the euphoria from a moment ago threatening to evaporate as thoughts of Grady chilled her arousal.

"No?" His brows furrowed in concern and he pulled away a few inches. Far enough that the air of the room cooled her heated skin. He brushed a lock of hair from her face with gentle fingers, his lips downturned and his voice soft with acceptance. "Oh, okay. I understand. If this is as much as you want tonight, do you also want me to leave so you can be alone?"

Her heart clenched. He thought she'd meant *no,* as in stop making love to her? A violent throng of cyborg haters beating down her door couldn't stop her from wanting every carnal delight he had to offer. Yet, even though his erection still pressed against her hip, he was willing to stop and walk away simply because she'd said *no.*

Everett Dean—the man who'd probably been told *no* and *you can't do that* and *stick to the rules* all his life and had ignored, brushed past, and crushed those obstacles to create himself into one of the most influential men in the world—had heard her *no* and thought it meant she no longer wished to continue their sexual intimacy. And had responded in the most gentlemanly, considerate manner possible.

Lots of women said *no* during sex and were ignored. Three men had intended to do this very thing to her a mere day ago. As a spy, she'd never had the choice to say *no*. But the one time she said it and hadn't meant it…

Betty cupped Everett's cheek, halting his retreat.

"You don't understand. I don't mean *no* as in *stop*. I meant it as *don't imitate that man*. You were only joking when you sounded like Detective Grady, but he is not welcome here." Her legs twined around Everett's and she glanced around the room, half afraid she might spot Grady lurking in the dark corners like a lecherous creep. "He's never been invited. He doesn't get to be here, in my apartment, in my bedroom, in my head. Not with me. Not with us."

"I'm sorry I made you think about him." Everett palmed her thigh, squeezing as if to reassure her, and claimed her lips in a slow kiss which quickly grew deep and passionate until they had to break away to gasp for air. He rested his forehead against hers, their lips a panting, desperate breath away. "Call me selfish, but I want to be the only man in your bedroom and your mind. At least for tonight. And preferably for the foreseeable future."

After another deep, soul-stealing kiss, he moved to kneel between her legs, unhooking her garter to slide her panties off, then spreading her thighs with his own. He made no other move. Merely gazed down at her body splayed and waiting for whatever he planned next.

She lay before him, covered only in her stockings and garters, leaving nothing to his imagination. Betty had long ago gotten over any pretense of modesty. Others seeing her naked didn't even make her blink. For so much of her adult life, her body had been merely a commodity used to trade for money or goods or information.

She'd never before felt so… unveiled and vulnerable. And not because her legs were spread, her womanly folds an open blossom for Everett to view. But because he was the first man to see her. To look at her and not see how he could use her to benefit himself, but to see her for the woman she was. A strange revelation, considering he still didn't know *what* she really was. But he kneeled before her like a knight before a queen, and his gaze drank her in, his expression one of utter wonder. He caressed her belly, thighs, calves, even the arches of her feet… his touch reverent, like she was a heavenly creature.

When he braced his hands behind her knees to spread her wider, then buried his face in her core, she ascended from being a mere creature of lust. Greater than a mortal being with unfulfilled desires coursing through her veins. More than a lost woman who'd walked the sordid path and stained her soul so it would never wash clean.

He moaned as he licked and kissed and sucked on her, worshipping her and immersing in her nectar like she was a baptismal fount. She'd never before felt so beautiful. She was art. She was muse. She was inspiration.

She was coming again.

"Everett!" Betty cried out his name, fisting his hair and arching against his tongue as he continued to wring more pleasure out of her. She quivered and convulsed as the molten lava in her veins became electric currents, zapping and zinging along her nerve endings. He clung to her, riding her storm, devouring her surge until the turbulence of her orgasm passed and she melted against the mattress.

"Delicious." He crawled back up her body, kissing and nuzzling along the way, until he could pull her into his arms again. Her lips quavered as he murmured against them, his voice the contented purr of a cat after a bowl of milk, speaking tender words. "You're so beautiful, Betty. So open and generous. So amazing and badass. I don't know what I did in a previous life to deserve this evening with you, but I'm so very grateful for it. So very grateful for the god who made you."

You made me. She didn't dare speak those words out loud, but the previous bitterness she'd felt about Everett being responsible for her cyborg status did not accompany the words in her head. In fact, only joy bubbled in her heart. A light, giddy, almost-drunk sensation followed Everett's words and caresses. She was beautiful in his eyes. Worthy. He demanded nothing she wasn't willing to give, and he returned her generosity with admiration and consideration she hadn't experienced in a long time, if at all.

It was the ultimate turn-on.

Betty giggled, which was uncharacteristic. She framed his face and he turned into her gloved palm before she pulled him down for more languid kisses. As if they had days, years, with nothing to contemplate but where next to place their lips upon one another. His body followed his mouth, settling against her side, one thigh between her legs, pressing her into the mattress with his weight.

Everett's broad hand traveled down her ribs, over her hip, and squeezed her buttock, grinding her against his erection. She nipped at his neck and reached for his cock, wrapping her fingers around it and pumping with the same maddening slowness he'd shown her earlier. He sucked in a breath and caught her bottom lip between his teeth, thrusting into her hand and gripping her ass cheek in that primal rhythm their bodies craved. His every motion and intent focused on her. A slow, methodical foreplay heightening her senses and setting her body so aflame she might never cool off.

She bucked against him, desire raging in her blood. She'd never wanted a man as much as she did this man, this moment. Wanted that primal connection, throbbed with readiness, slick with arousal. "Everett, while I love all this foreplay, I need you inside me. Now."

"I can't." He buried his face in the crook of her neck and groaned with regret.

Her blood tempered. "Can't or won't?"

"Both." He lifted his face to hers, a self-effacing half-smile on his lips. "I don't have any condoms on me. My pilot, in a deplorable lack of planning, did not pack any in my bugout bag. Nor did he leave me the funds to purchase any."

Betty's laugh burst from her lungs. She tried to stifle it, which turned it into a prolonged snort. Everett's eyes widened in shock at her reaction and she flashed him a wide smile, grateful for once for her cyborg status.

"I can't get pregnant. I… had a miscarriage when I was younger and it… it messed me up." A lie, but she couldn't tell him her uterus had been removed during her cyborg transition. Neither could she admit her system siphoned away all bacteria and viruses. "And I won't—I mean, I'm clean. No diseases."

"You're… really okay going without?" He pulled her hand from his cock. "I'm okay if you prefer to stop here. If we don't go any further, this is still the loveliest evening I've ever enjoyed, and I'm perfectly content."

"But I'm not." She slid a leg along his, loving the way his crisp curls tickled her smooth flesh. "I'm pretty sure I demanded you be inside me, pronto."

He rolled her onto her back and settled between her thighs. He pulled her hand to his lips, eyebrows lifted in challenge. "And I said I wanted you wearing nothing but your garters. That includes these."

Using only his teeth and tongue, he removed her gloves. Fear speared through her haze of arousal as he kissed and licked her bare fingers, sucking them into his mouth and nibbling their sensitive pads. Her finger datajack was firmly recessed, but what if he noticed? He didn't say anything, and soon moved on to her wrists and the sensitive inside of her elbow. She relaxed back into the fog of desire, exhaling a long sigh for having dodged a bullet.

When his cock pressed at her entrance, Betty nearly cried out, so ready to be filled by him. He thrust into her welcoming heat, and they set a swift pace, rocking and grinding together. She wrapped her legs around his torso and he moaned in her mouth, his tongue dancing against hers. Then he lifted to look in her eyes as her pleasure crested yet again, her body clenching his with each plunge as if to pull him under as she drowned in the tide of pleasure. He watched her face as he continued pumping. She gasped and keened, clinging to him as her entire body convulsed and thrashed. His gaze never wavered until his own release hit and he roared, bucked once more, tensed, and then collapsed on her.

Their breaths mingled as they floated down from their crescendo. Everett rolled to his back, taking her with him so their legs tangled and she listened his heartbeat as it calmed. He rested his chin atop her head and his arms tightened in a hug. Her eyelids dipped, the euphoric mix of dopamine—which she was grateful her cybernetic systems did not siphon—relaxed her muscles and Everett's body heat lulled her further into utter tranquility.

She drifted in a languid state of half-sleep, vaguely aware of him removing the remainder of her clothes and tucking her beside him under the sheets. The intimate cocoon of his care eased her into deep sleep, dotted with sensual dreams of Everett.

He'd wanted to be the only man she thought of for the foreseeable future, huh?

Wish granted.

Chapter Sixteen

"Damn, I don't think that was a weed." Everett stared at the delicate flower clasped between his two filthy fingers. It lay like a frail damsel, having fainted in reaction to his manhandling. He glanced around to see if his mishap had been witnessed, then tried to tuck the poor thing back into its mulchy location before moving on to the next flowerbed encircling the grounds of the Greater Broad Ripple Public Library.

Every muscle in his body burned, even some he hadn't known existed. His back throbbed from leaning forward all morning, weeding overgrown flower beds. His hands ached from plucking more weeds than he thought could possibly exist in the world, much less in one small library's landscaping.

He might very well have worked his fingers to the bone, just as he'd offered to do for Betty.

The fact made him smile as much as the beautiful weather. The day was sunny, without the previous overbearing humidity thanks to a late-night rain, and lazy clouds in the sky offered occasional shade. The neighborhood was popular and busy, but the library was a peaceful, subdued oasis amid the bustle and noise. In spite of the aching protest of his muscles, he reveled in the placid atmosphere of this morning.

Granted, the pleasant weather had very little influence on his good mood. A night spent in the arms of a certain sexy librarian got that credit.

Everett sat back on his heels and smiled at the memory of last night. He'd been as nervous as a teen on a first date while showering. Somehow, standing naked in a spot where Betty also habitually stood naked—even if that bathroom looked like someone had vomited Pepto-Bismol tiles and Gary Cooper movie posters—had been stirring in a way a man of his age should be immune to. He'd been hyper-aware of her last night while sitting next to her at her kitchen table. She'd looked everywhere but at him. Her hands had been hummingbirds darting about, never settling. The longing in her eyes a siren's call he'd been unable to resist.

Maybe he confused his underlying fear and dread for his own life with feelings of desire. Or maybe his desire had been amplified by the worry about what their individual futures would bring. Regardless, he'd wanted to lose himself in Betty's arms and lips. Wanted to drown in something sincere and unadulterated. Wanted to be part of something beautiful. Wanted to give all that back in return. Had he known how amazing it would be, how responsive and utterly delectable Betty was, he would have thrown caution, the attempt on his life, and his ruined career to the wind the first moment he'd walked in the library door and instead set to seducing her.

Everett touched two fingers to his lips, ignoring their dirt cover and mulch scent and instead remembering Betty's sweet flavor coating his tongue. She'd been gloriously uninhibited last night, yet also modest. Spread wide open with nothing to obstruct his view of her womanly beauty, she had still worn her gloves. Had caressed him and scraped her nails along his skin through the satin fabric without seeming to even consider removing them. And she'd looked shocked when he'd insisted on it.

He shrugged off her little quirk, then stopped. A desire-addled memory popped up, scraped clean and more transparent in the light of day. He'd removed her gloves and nibbled on her fingers last night. One fingertip had been rigid, tough and unyielding beneath his teeth like a large callous. A large callous with corners. And, while the rest of her fingers had tasted of pizza sauce and cheese, that one had tasted vaguely of metal and ozone. In fact, it had tasted like Preditech's design lab smelled.

Like cyborgs.

His heart seized for a moment, then continued at a breakneck pace. Was Betty a cyborg? Was this more *wacky shit* he should worry about? Each of the numerous times his thoughts had come to a dead end where his life, future, and Preditech were concerned, they'd turned to the more pleasant contemplation of this woman. Vibrant, generous, beautiful—apparently possibly a cyborg—Betty. It had been a long time since any woman had piqued his interest. And the one who finally did could be a product of his own company. What did it signify? Was it coincidence they'd met, or some reason far more nefarious?

"Care for lemonade?" Betty's bright voice trilled over his nerves, raising hairs on his arms even in the morning's warmth. Like remnants of a drug, images of last night played in his mind, elbowing out his paranoia. Maybe she was a cyborg, but that didn't mean she would go rogue and kill him. Not now. He'd been around her for too long, and had been vulnerable too many times. If that was the plan he'd stumbled into, he'd already be dead.

"Ev-um, Clark? Are you okay?"

Her voice was closer, alarmed. He shook his head and stood to face her, arching to stretch his aching muscles and rubbing the back of his neck. "I'm fine, Betty. Just… contemplating life, I guess."

She stood like an angelic vixen, wrapped in a black halter dress with a red cherry pattern and a plunging sweetheart neckline which emphasized her voluptuous curves, most especially the rounded tops of her bountiful breasts. Her red hair was piled high and secured with a polka dot scarf, leaving her graceful neck bare and beckoning for tender kisses. Her hands encased in black lace gloves to the wrist.

He itched to remove the gloves—the entire outfit—in the same manner he had last night.

"Contemplating life, huh?" Her smile was genuine as she settled her weight on one hip. "Come up with any interesting revelations?"

The world and worry faded away, leaving only the vision before him and his rising desire to lose himself in her arms again. She was a peaceful oasis amid the battle that raged in his life. In his soul. He didn't dare admit to her that his only realization was the fact he was so strongly attracted to her.

So he shrugged and tried to act cool. Instead, he blurted. "Only that I want you again."

He slapped his hand to his face and Betty giggled. When he peered through his fingers at her, her fingers toyed with her lips, contemplating the ground with an absentminded gaze, like he'd done earlier. She blushed like a woman new to being flirted with, and damn if that wasn't sexy as hell.

Then she lifted her gaze to his and the heat of desire banked in its depths stole his breath away.

Betty cleared her throat and toyed with the fabric of her skirt. "Well, I'm tempted to say a few more hours of weeding might help you with your revelations, but that would be a lie and you're already almost finished." She canted her head in empathy, and her voice softened. "How about you come in for a glass of lemonade and some cucumber sandwiches and we'll further explore your revelation?"

"I'll take you up on that offer." He smiled, but despair welled up his throat. As much as he'd love another tryst with Betty, he needed to focus on his current predicament. And as much as he'd love to have Betty's help in his current predicament, he wasn't sure she could be that friend. Wasn't sure it was even fair to lay that responsibility at her feet. In spite of the fact she'd been an amazing lover, and even if she could be his friend and confidante, he didn't want her life to be in danger. Antony had already sacrificed his life. Everett didn't dare ask anyone else to take such risks. He shoved his hands in his pockets and stared at the bright yellow flowers puckered among the green foliage along the sidewalk. Oh, to be cheerful little flowers with no worries and nothing to do but soak up sunshine and bask in rain showers. And hope a careless human didn't pull you out of your comfy mulch bed.

But if he were a flower, then he never would have chased his dream of cybernetic advancement. Which meant he never would have experienced a lot of things, both good and bad, the most meaningful at the moment being the fact he never would have met Betty. Betty, who hadn't looked at him with that prospector's gleam he'd so often seen in his business and social circles. Like he was a meal ticket or a prized bauble to inspire envy among the upper crust. She'd known him as Clark the homeless man and accepted him without pity, judgment, or expectation. Now that she knew him as Everett Dean, she looked at him the same as she always had.

A smart man would do anything he could to earn that look from a good woman like Betty. People could say what they wanted about him, but no one ever claimed Everett was stupid.

He brushed the dirt off his hands and turned her with a palm at the small of her back, leaning down to murmur in her ear and noticing her skin pebble when he did. "Lemonade first. Then we'll see what else we're in the mood for."

She slanted a sultry smile in his direction. Their morning had been rushed because neither had set a wakeup alarm, and they'd had little time to discuss the ramifications of last night. This morning-after could have been all kinds of awkward and unsettled. Instead, it had been rife with shy glances and coy smiles, the brush of hands and shoulders, the way she held her breath whenever he leaned closer to talk to her… it all proved he hadn't manhandled their blooming relationship as badly as he had the library flower beds. It proved there was still hope.

They entered through the back door, and Everett washed his hands and the dirt prints off his face while Betty poured two glasses of lemonade, minus any gin. Then she ushered him to another library reading nook. Near enough to the front door Betty could quickly greet any patrons, the single tufted velvet settee in a lush emerald green was situated at an angle to maximize its privacy.

Unless someone walked directly up to them, they would be practically invisible.

Betty slid out of her cherry-red pumps and curled her feet under as she settled onto the couch. Everett leaned back and stretched his arm along the top, his fingers tracing circles on her bare shoulder. She leaned into the hollow space at his side. After a few quiet sips, he set their glasses on a side table.

"Everett, last night…" She opened up the conversation, then paused, her eyes searching his.

"Was wonderful." He finished for her. "And I hope we get to enjoy many more like it, if that's also what you want."

A sad smile graced her lips. "There's a *but* in there, isn't there?"

He nodded. "But, I have no job or money." Damn how that admission rankled. Mere days ago, he'd owned the world. Now he couldn't even afford a brazen attitude. "I have no future. And being with me puts you in danger."

She rested her hand lightly over his heart. "I've been in danger before. It doesn't frighten me."

"You're a braver soul than me." He chuckled as he lifted her gloved fingers to his lips. "Because my feelings for you terrify me. I've never felt like this with another woman."

He pulled her forward and lifted her to straddle his lap, spreading her skirt and netted layer beneath to minimize wrinkles. Then he kissed her. Slow, languid kisses as if they had years of peaceful Sunday afternoons filled with tea cozies, planters of succulents, and T.S. Elliot poems. A leisurely exploration of each other. Their flavors and sounds. Which nibbles and licks brought forth the softest sighs. How their mouths fit perfectly together when slanted a certain angle. The tantalizing slide of tongue along tongue which they both felt to their core if their mutual moans and clutching was any indication.

He carefully stripped away her gloves while he nibbled and sucked along her neck. She tilted her head to the side to give him better access and arched on a moan when he found a particularly sweet spot. Once her gloves were removed, he switched his attention to her fingers. Like last night, he nibbled and sucked, stopping when he tasted the faint metal tang again.

One hand clasping hers, his other cupping the back of her neck, he kissed her once more before pulling back enough to look at her face. Her eyes were heavy-lidded with arousal, her lips plumped, and a delightful flush on her cheeks. She looked like a dream, and he hated that he was about to ruin it. But he needed confirmation.

In one swift motion, he pinched her finger with one hand to pop open her datajack and pressed against the scarred skin covering the access panel at the base of her skull with the other. "Betty? Are you a cyborg?"

Stupid question because the proof was right there, but he wanted her to admit it. As expected, she blinked in shock and jerked back away from his body, raising up as if to jump off both his lap and the settee. Her brows furrowed and betrayal replaced the desire in her eyes. She tried to pull her hand from his, but he held firm. He softened his voice, hoping it would soothe her fears. "You know I'm okay with it, right? Your secret is safe with me."

Her face crumpled in panic and she jerked away again. This time, he let her go. Holding her captive wouldn't help anything, especially his claim of safety, and she might throat punch him for it. She backed away, out of reach, until a bookcase stopped her retreat. Arms wide and ready to defend herself, she gasped for air, her gaze darting around the room until it finally locked on his. Everett remained seated, his hands open and resting palms up on the settee to appear as nonthreatening as possible. She was a wild animal backed into a corner; he didn't dare exacerbate her fight or flight reaction.

"H-how... How did you know?"

Her fingerjack was still open, and he'd recognized the texture of her access panel beneath her skin like a mother knew her own child. Before he could answer, she glanced at her finger and huffed a laugh lacking any humor. "Stupid question, I guess. Of course you'd recognize me. You made me."

"No." He shook his head, wanting more than anything to pull her into his arms to comfort her and knowing it was the last thing he should do. "I didn't *make* you, Betty. Yes, I designed the cybernetic systems inside you—"

"How is that not making me?" She shouted, her voice hoarse with pain, her chest heaving with emotion.

He sighed and shook his head, keeping his voice calm and steady, his gaze never leaving hers. "Betty, only *you* can make you. You have my cybernetic systems inside you, yes. But they don't determine *who* you are any more than your choice of clothes, your hair color, or DNA."

"Society would disagree."

"Can we agree society is fucked up? Just because it wants to define *what* you are, it doesn't get a say in *who* you are. Only you can do that."

Her shoulders relaxed and the panic in her eyes lessened. He leaned forward, bracing his elbows on his knees. "Betty, you know I'm on your side, don't you? I want you to be safe and to live out your life as you desire, just as much as I want the same for myself. You being a cybernetic individual doesn't change my opinion of you. Nor does it affect what I feel for you."

She looked down at her finger and retracted the datajack. Dare he hope she believed his words? When she looked up again, she lifted an eyebrow, her lips in a stubborn line. "And what do you feel for me, Everett Dean?"

He met her gaze without hesitation. "I feel you a beautiful, vibrant woman. That you hold a wealth of empathy and kindness, which I'm grateful to be on the receiving end of because you're also not a pushover and are capable of putting a man in his place in no uncertain terms. If I had *made* the woman of my dreams, I wouldn't have done half as well as the woman you made yourself into."

She narrowed her eyes as if she thought he was full of bull. He scratched his jawline and blew out a breath. "My feelings run deeper for you than they have any other woman."

One manicured eyebrow arched above an eye. "That's a pretty lame confession of love."

He chuckled, but his heart withered a bit. Did she honestly expect him to declare his love? Because he couldn't do that. Not and be honest with her. Not yet. "It's not a confession of love. We've only known each other a few days. Love doesn't happen that quickly, right?"

Hell, maybe it did. What did he know about the emotion?

Betty tried to cover her laugh, but was unsuccessful. She smiled at him and shrugged. "It happens all the time in romance novels. But then again, they're also…"

"Fiction." He finished for her. "Look, I won't profess that I love you just because I think it's what you want to hear. But I confess that I'm intensely attracted to you and have been from the start. I'm attracted to your beauty, both inside and out. I like you, Betty."

He scrubbed a hand through his hair. "And I know I'm the last man in the world you should be with, not with all the shit going on around me. For your own self-preservation, you should kick me to the curb and call the authorities to take me away. It's the only way to keep you safe, because I don't have the strength to walk away on my own."

Betty straightened her shoulders and brushed at something on her skirt. Then she slowly approached him, her voice quiet even in the library's silence. "Yes, Everett. I'm a cyborg. I was homeless and easily lured in with promises of being a next-level badass government spy. My uterus was removed. I was fitted with this"—she wiggled her datajack finger—"Given a hyper-fast CPU, all manner of software programs, and trained in a variety of self-defense and combat styles."

She eased down on the edge of the settee next to him, not touching him, her body tense and ready to flee. Grief and regret filled her eyes. "Rather than overseas assignments, my targets were government officials and staff members. I assume I slept with them and downloaded proof of treasonous acts. Which makes me both a whore and a traitor myself." Her gaze dropped to her lap and she fiddled with the hem of her skirt. "After a few years of that, I carved out my modem with a kitchen knife and a compact mirror, and ran away to the smallest neighborhood in the biggest city my money could get me to, and tried to lose myself in anonymity."

Everett listened to her confession with a growing mix of

horror and outrage. The thoughts flying through his head scattered like debris in a hurricane, so much of what she'd experienced explaining why she was the woman he'd come to know. He was both grateful and sickened by what she'd been through.

And livid at how his cybernetic systems had been so bastardized.

Rage entered the violent mix of emotions churning in his chest. Someone had taken what he'd created to help better humanity—and, yes, his pocketbook—and had turned it ugly and intrusive. Someone had transformed cyborgs into the monsters society assumed they were. Antony driving the plane into the ground, Betty seducing for government secrets… Someone was using cyborgs for their own personal gain.

Someone like… *Hawks.*

"Hawks who?" Betty asked, pulling him out of his own thoughts.

Acid burned his blood at what atrocities that man was apparently capable of. "Richard Hawks, Director of the DCO. Ever heard of him or talked to him?"

She shook her head. "I know who Richard Hawks is, but have never had an occasion to be around him."

"So, he wasn't the one giving you orders?"

She chewed on her bottom lip, her brows furrowed. "I don't know who gave me orders. I don't remember any of it. What my orders were or who gave them or what intel I collected. It's like I'm programmed to dump it all once my mission was complete. I'd begin an *assignment* and then wake up in my bedroom the next morning."

"How do you know you slept with them? And infiltrated government secrets?"

She shrugged. "Common sense. I have a datajack fingertip built for only one purpose. And men don't look at you and touch you the way my *dates* did me. Not unless your consent has already been decided for you."

Everett pulled her hands into his, waiting for her to jerk them back, or punch him for his part in her cybernetic experience. She did neither. "Betty. I'm so sorry for what you've suffered. I never built my systems to be used like that... to take away your autonomy. I just... wish I'd had the forethought to anticipate how my systems would be abused."

His shoulders slumped with the realization he'd been played from the very beginning. The design had been his, but Hawks had been the driving force behind it. The puppet master pulling all the strings. Everett had been the marionette. The mouthpiece. The performing monkey. Hawks had distracted him with dollar signs, and Everett had gladly done what he'd been asked.

Guess he wasn't as smart as he thought.

Betty squeezed his hands. "Heroes always expect the villains to play by the rules. And are always surprised when the villains don't. You couldn't have known all the possible ways someone with no scruples could twist your creations."

She leaned forward and kissed him lightly, but with enough intent he knew she'd forgiven him. Then she pulled back to gaze in his eyes. "For what it's worth, I'm sorry for what you've been through, too. But I'm also glad you're here with me."

"Me, too." Everett's heart grew wings, and he pulled her onto his lap to kiss her thoroughly. She sighed softly and leaned into him, deepening the kiss.

When Everett palmed her thigh underneath the crinoline of her skirt, the phone rang. Betty jerked back, confusion and frustration warring on her face as she climbed off his lap, murmuring. "No one ever calls here."

She hastened to her desk, Everett following close behind. Maybe it was an after-effect of his recent emotional upheaval, but he wanted Betty in eyesight. In his arms was preferable.

Donning her customer service expression, she answered the

phone. "Greater Broad Ripple Public Library. How can I help you?"

"Is this Betty Hayworth? Formerly known as Luann Mathison?" The man's voice reached Everett where he stood several feet away. Something about it set his nerves on edge. Something about it was familiar. He stepped closer to the desk.

Betty's eyes shot wide and alarm. Fortunately, the speaker couldn't see her reaction proving him right. She inhaled and spoke as if the man irritated her. "This is Betty the librarian. Is there anything specific you need?"

"Indeed there is. I assume Everett Dean is still sniffing around your skirts, especially after you fucked him."

Betty gasped and Everett tensed, his heart racing. He recognized that voice now. He shook his head, but couldn't negate the truth of who called.

Richard Hawks. Everett mouthed the name to Betty.

She frowned, her voice ice and her tone steel. "Sir, your speculation and language are both unwelcome. Don't call back."

Hawks replied before she could hang up. "*Tsk*, Betty. *What would the neighbors think?*"

Betty paused, her expression blanking to an emotionless mask, her eyes unfocused, pupils dilated. The same reaction when Grady had said that phrase. And when it had tumbled from her own mouth before that. She was a blank page waiting for words to fill it. She was a blinking cursor, waiting for the next keystroke.

Shit! That was it!

Everett's blood froze in his veins as clarity detonated in his brain. That phrase had sparked familiarity… because it was a phrase he had for a short period of time programmed into specialized systems. A hard-coded override command meant as a failsafe for malfunctioning systems. A system reboot, so to speak. Cyborg Ctrl-Alt-Del.

He'd once mentioned it to Hawks over drinks. The bastard

had obviously used it to his full advantage, whereas Everett had forgotten about it. And now Betty was at the mercy of whatever command she'd be given.

Everett opened his mouth, but Hawks beat him to it. "Kill Everett Dean."

The phone line went dead. Betty's eyes focused on him, her pupils fixating on him like lasers. Her face hard and stark, missing all the soft emotions she'd shown the past few days. Gone was her ready smile. Gone was her humor. Gone was her passion. She stepped in his direction, her body language that of a lioness on the hunt and he was her prey.

His heart beat against his chest to escape. He'd never been so terrified, even when jumping out of a plummeting jet. Betty was fierce in a combat situation, like the altercation with three drunks. And they hadn't pulled their punches like Everett would do instinctively because he didn't want to hurt her. Under Hawks's command, she wouldn't hesitate or let compassion get in the way. Everett was well and truly fucked. "Betty, you have to fight that order."

His voice cracked, lacking any strength or firmness. Probably because he had to speak around his testicles which had retracted into his throat. He even held his hands out in front of him, as if that could stop her. Betty shook her head, her gaze never leaving his, her voice strained. "I can't. I've never been able to resist or fight… and believe me, I've been ordered to do worse than this."

Everett stepped back. "You have to try, darlin'." Even Grady's shitty twang didn't give her pause. "I'm no match for you, and I don't want to hurt you in the process."

Tears streamed down her face as the back of his legs hit a loveseat and he tumbled onto its cushions, trapping him in a tufted prison. But she never ceased her approach. Shaking her head, she screeched, gasping for air, her hands fisted around her skirt, her words forced through a clenched jaw. "Run, dammit. Run away from here. Far away. Somewhere I'll never find you."

All panic whooshed from Everett's body, leaving an odd sense of peace. Even under orders to kill him, her compassion reigned. He shook his head and sat up, refusing to cower in his last moments. Meeting his fate head-on. "No. I'm not going to run and I'm not going to leave you. Not when you're stuck doing the dirty work of a spineless asshole. Not when you're being forced against your will."

"Then you're going to have to kill me." She sobbed as she reached him. "Because I have to kill you."

In a blink, she'd clutched his throat and shoved him back against the cushions. He grabbed at her hands and fingers to loosen her grip, but she was too strong, her cybernetic systems making her muscles superhuman. Everett gasped for air, his heartbeat pounding in his ears, his vision blurring and turning dark while Betty's tormented face hovered over him. Instead of a panicked struggle for air, a strange calm wrapped him. He gripped the bodice of her dress and pulled her in for a brief, but deep, kiss. When he pulled back, he rested his forehead on hers and tried to talk past the clamp of fingers around his throat.

"Betty. What would the neighbors think?" The blackness swept over him but he shoved it aside for one more heartbeat. "You don't ever have to obey that command again."

He fell back into oblivion, weightless and content, death claiming him.

A bright light slashed through the dark void. He jerked to sit up, gasping for air and coughing, wiping tears from his eyes and swatting at the pair of hands fussing with him. After several moments struggling to make sense of what was happening, his vision cleared enough for him to see the figure of a man standing above a lump of black fabric dotted with red cherries. Betty. Betty lay on the ground in a heap as if she'd fainted.

Or the hulk of a man had killed her.

Rage gave Everett strength, and he gripped the seat to launch himself at the stranger, but two hands on his shoulders held him back. Then a voice. A familiar voice spoke in his ear. "Everett, it's okay. You're okay. You're both safe."

Everett turned to see his former exec on the loveseat's arm. He blinked. Maybe this was a dream. Or the afterlife.

His throat hurt from the recent strangulation, but he managed to choke out a few words. "Eve. Thought you were dead."

Chapter Seventeen

Betty woke slowly, the light peeking through the seam of her eyelids brighter than normal, painfully so. Had she left her curtains open? Had she fallen asleep under a lamp?

Her body ached, and not in a good, night-in-Everett's-arms kind of way. The antiseptic smell of the room and the cold metal gurney underneath her registered on her senses, jarring her further from her dreamless sleep and into wakefulness. The muted drone of what should have been morning traffic clarified into whispered voices. Voices that weren't Everett. This wasn't her bed, and those weren't welcome guests.

Or were they? She honestly didn't know because she couldn't remember.

Tears burned in her eyes. How many mornings as a so-called spy had she woken up with the same sense of amnesia? Hours of the past evening simply gone from her head, like someone had scooped it out with a melon-baller, leaving an emptiness she couldn't explain or fill.

She rolled away from the annoying light and voices, but was stopped by straps at her wrists and forehead. Her heart jumped.

She was tied down. Where? By who? What had happened? What had she done? *Who* had she done?

Where was Everett?

"Doc, she's awake." A deep voice beyond her head spoke, chilling her blood. An unknown man, a doctor, restraints… This couldn't be good. Panic set in, but the shot of adrenaline was quickly filtered from her system. Her cybernetics kept her composed in a crisis, but they couldn't answer any of the questions clanging in her brain.

"Shhh, Betty. Calm down." The woman's voice at her side was familiar. Where had she—

Eve Myer.

Betty opened her eyes and spotted the woman's rich auburn hair and toffee brown eyes in her peripheral. Eve sat nearby, but not close enough to allow contact should Betty's bonds slip. Eve smiled as if she were offering a cup of tea and finger sandwiches, not addressing a woman who was strapped down. "This is a safe place. We mean you no harm."

Eve's efforts to calm her had the opposite effect. Not trusting her voice, Betty glanced meaningfully at her arm restraints, then glared at Eve, who had the grace to look contrite. "Those are everyone's safety. Ours and yours."

"Just what—" Betty's voice cracked. She frowned and cleared her throat. "Just what are they keeping all of us safe from, *hon*?"

Eve mushed her lips together as if spreading her lip gloss. "Honestly, from you."

Betty lifted an eyebrow. "Librarians scare you that much?"

Eve shook her head, sadness creeping into her eyes. "Betty, we know you're a cyborg. And your secret is safe with us."

Where had Betty heard that promise before?

Eve continued, leaning a tad closer. "I'm serious when I say that. The man I love is a cyborg. You're in a lab designed to help cyborgs. We're trying to fight whoever it is who is killing cyborgs—"

"Good for you. But that doesn't explain why I'm here." Her words were terse and clipped. Whatever patience and understanding Betty usually had was nonexistent today. She didn't care about Eve's love life or personal jihad. Betty wanted out, away from here, back to her home and the safety of her little library. And where was Everett?

"Her readings are too high, darlin'. Let me try." A man's voice that lacked Grady's twang moved to flank her, standing close enough she didn't have to strain to see him. He was tall, with broad shoulders, an overgrown salt-and-pepper buzz cut, and muscles for miles beneath his black shirt and jeans. He was handsome in a blue-collar sort of way. But if he thought to intimidate her with his sheer strength, he was in for a shock. She'd trained for hostage situations like this, not that she'd ever needed to use those skills before.

"Hi, Betty. I'm Adam, the cyborg Eve mentioned. I was once a police officer." That explained why his deep voice was calm and soothing, like what Grady often used with her, but without his condescension. Adam tilted his head in such a way a dull red shadow appeared behind the nearly-inhuman blue iris of his left eye. An unquestionable sign of cybernetics, no doubt to prove he told the truth. And likely to gain her trust. "I was injured in the line of duty, so I'm alpha-phase. Which probably makes you beta-phase, doesn't it? Trained spy and assassin. I understand why you're so guarded."

Adam gave her a few moments to respond, but she merely stared at him, her lips in a mulish line. Yes, she was being petulant. But he wasn't helping with her *high readings,* whatever that meant. He smiled, seemingly not at all upset with her obstinacy. "This isn't an interrogation, Betty. We're not your enemy."

She strained against the bonds for a moment to contradict his claim. He chuckled like they'd shared a joke. "I get it. And I hope you won't need those much longer."

"Betty, how much do you remember about yesterday?" Eve's brows furrowed and she mashed her lips again. The woman better never play poker because she had some massive tells. Before a terse response could pop out of Betty's mouth, she considered the question. Because, honestly, the missing hours alarmed her. That, and the fact she still hadn't seen Everett.

"What time is it?" She croaked, swallowing past her sore throat.

"You mean, what day?" Empathy crept into Eve's eyes. "Betty, it's Saturday. Well, it's three A.M. on Saturday. We picked you up at the library yesterday before lunchtime. You've been out for nearly fifteen hours."

Betty's gut hollowed. She'd lost more than half a day. Exactly like her years as a spy, she'd lost massive hours of time, as if—poof!—they had never existed. But it had been years since she'd suffered such an episode. Why have one now? And where was Everett? Why wasn't he here with his former executive and her boy toy? Had they—

Betty's heart lurched. Surely they hadn't killed him. What would be the benefit of that? Maybe something had happened before they'd arrived. Why couldn't she remember anything?

Her last memory was sitting with Everett, sipping lemonade on the couch. He'd... he'd called her a cyborg. And she'd panicked. Even knowing he wouldn't judge her or hate her, she'd been ready—desperate—to claw her way to safety. An instinct built from years of having to hide. But she didn't have to hide with Everett. He'd professed his... *like*... for her. Betty nearly smiled at that memory, her body warming with the same powerful emotion for him. Then she'd confessed everything, and the *like* in his eyes had never wavered, even knowing she'd whored her body out to who-knows-how-many people. Then they'd... kissed... and then... a phone call from... a voice. She hadn't recognized it, but it had felt… familiar. A voice she'd been shocked to hear, especially on a phone because… because she'd always heard it directly in her head. Her handler. Betty winced as she struggled to piece it together. Everett had said a name. The name of the person on the phone. The person who'd—

"Hawks." She croaked, her voice hoarse with shock. "Richard Hawks."

"You mean DCO Director Richard Hawks?" Adam nodded as if she'd confirmed his suspicions. Damn, so much for her hostage training. Some spy she was, giving them information they hadn't even asked for. Bitterness soured on her tongue.

Adam leaned closer, his expression filled with concern. "Betty, do you know you have an override command? There's a phrase encoded into your CPU you are hardwired to obey, regardless of your personal choice."

"Wh-what do you mean?"

Adam shifted as if uncomfortable with what he was about to say. Eve reached over Betty's prone body and squeezed his arm before looking at her. "If you're given a specific phrase, then you must obey the command which comes after. It was meant as a system reboot of sorts, but we think it's been abused. We think Richard Hawks used that phrase on you at the library. Chances are likely he's used that phrase on you when you were in service. When you were a spy. And he's likely done the same with other beta-phase spy cyborgs."

Betty blinked, struggling to understand. Or rather, struggling to fully grasp the ramifications of it all. Was it true? She had an override to her own wishes? Her own self agency? Betty swallowed, fear and anguish seesawing in her gut until her stomach heaved, threatening to spill. Training be damned, she needed answers. "So… you think he's the one who commanded me to sleep with my targets? H-how do you know that? How do you know I was ordered to…to fuck my targets? I barely know that, and I was there. I was there, and I can't remember any of it! Why can't I remember any of those nights! AND WHERE IS EVERETT?"

Her voice cracked with the force of her screams, tears streaming down her cheeks like a rainstorm on a windowpane. Wrong image. Like the overflow of hot lava as years of frustration and fear and worry bubbled to the surface. The memories and memory gaps from her escort-spy days a volcano erupting. What horrible things had she been commanded to do? How black was her soul?

Adam and Eve exchanged cryptic glances, then Adam coughed. "Betty, when we arrived at the library, you were strangling Everett."

She stared at him, willing him to declare this was a horrible joke. No way she would try to strangle Everett. He was her… he liked her… and she… liked him in return. When Adam said nothing, she swallowed past the cauldron of emotions lodged in her throat, her voice barely a whisper. "But you stopped me, right? You saved him. He's alive."

"Is that what you remember?"

What a stupid-ass question. She seethed, her fists and teeth clenched. "I don't remember anything." She practically snarled. "Remember?"

Another cryptic glance exchanged above her. Eve turned away and Adam crossed his arms over his chest, taking a deep breath as if bracing to deliver bad news. Betty braced as well, fresh tears springing to her eyes when he shook his head. All her body language programming confirmed he was about to tell the truth. "Betty, you were ordered to kill him. Do you remember that?"

She shook her head as best she could with the restraints still in place, tears falling down her temples and her lips quivering. All fight and anger drained from her limbs, leaving her a hopeless vessel of remorse. She'd killed Everett? Because she'd been ordered to? Had she ever been ordered to kill before? She'd always assumed she'd slept with her targets, but had never considered the possibility she'd murdered them instead. So much for the glimmer of hope she could build a life with Everett. This wasn't a romance novel; it was a horror story, and she the villain who bit it in the end. And running away to carve out a meager life somewhere else? She didn't deserve it. The sins of her forgotten past were too numerous and too unforgiveable. Maybe Adam and Eve were here to decommission her. Permanently. Betty didn't have any fight left in her to object.

"Quit wasting my time." Her whisper was as watery as the silent sobs she choked back. She closed her eyes, and waited for the end to come. "Get it over with."

Footsteps sounded in her ears and bodies jostled above her, bumping the gurney. She steeled for what was to come. But then gentle hands cupped her cheeks and fingers wiped at her streaming tears. "Betty, sweetheart, don't cry." A man's hoarse voice was right above her face, breath warming her wet cheeks. "I'm very much alive."

Everett!

Her eyelids flew open, and she moaned at the sight of his handsome face. His brows were furrowed with concern, and lov —er, like—shone in his eyes. His throat was mottled purple with bruises and his voice was strained from being crushed. More tears gushed from her eyes. "Everett, your poor throat! I'm so sorry, I... I don't remember what happened, but I didn't... I would never have done that willingly."

"Shhhh. I know." He kissed her, in spite of her runny nose and attempted murder. Then he rested he forehead against hers. "It's my fault. This is all my fault."

Another sweet, lingering kiss, then he pulled back to look her in the eyes. "I designed your cybernetic systems with a reboot triggered by a voice command. It was meant to be a failsafe for malfunctions we couldn't anticipate. Unfortunately, I couldn't anticipate humanity's talent for twisting a good thing to serve a selfish purpose. Especially greedy bastards like Richard Hawks."

He sat back and squeezed her hand, his face contorted with regret. "And you are the one who had to suffer my lack of foresight. I'm the one who is so sorry. Can you ever forgive me?"

Laughter burst from her throat, bright and jubilant like a noonday sun when the rain clouds part. Everett looked ready to throw himself on a pyre as punishment for his wrongdoings. Everett, with handprint bruises along his neck and bloodshot eyes from her attempted strangulation, was riddled with guilt for the choices he'd made years before having known her. She smiled up at him, her heart lighter in her chest than she'd ever thought it could be. She was either truly happy for the first time in her life, or she was having a heart attack.

"Everett, you've done nothing that warrants my forgiveness. And I've suffered far more from my own lack of foresight than anyone else's, including yours. How about we consider ourselves even and move forward?"

"Together?"

The hope in his voice nearly made her laugh again. It sounded like how she felt. "Yes. Together. I'd like that very much."

He moved to unbuckle her restraints, but Adam stopped him. "Betty, you were ordered to kill Everett." His voice was dark with wariness. "And your target is within your grasp. How do you feel right now?"

Would she default back to her command and try again? Would they stop her if she did? Was it worth the risk to be free of her bonds so Everett could hold her? She stared at him and waited. Waited for the desire, the need, the undeniable urge to kill him. But all she felt was the overwhelming wish to be in his arms. To tell him she loved him.

Betty turned her attention to Adam. Hopefully he would hear

the truth in her words. "I feel normal. But please stick close to me, just in case. If the kill command is lingering in my CPU, I don't want to find out the hard way. Please keep Everett safe from me."

Adam considered her for a few moments before nodding, as if he'd come to a decision. Then he unbuckled the strap at her forehead before moving to her wrists. He glanced at her, a lopsided smirk on his face. "I'll keep a sharp eye on you both. So no hanky-panky."

"I make no promises." Betty shrugged as she sat up and massaged her wrists while Adam worked on the straps at her ankles. She smiled at Everett who hovered by Adam as if waiting for his go-ahead. "Especially if hanky-panky is involved."

Adam's gaze cut to Everett, who chuckled and held his palms out in surrender. "I wouldn't say *no* to some hanky-panky. Not with a woman as beautiful as Betty."

Adam glanced at Eve and grumbled, trying to hide his smile. "Can't say I don't understand your point."

He flicked the final strap and swung Betty's legs around so they dangled off the gurney. Then Adam stepped out of the way as Everett surged forward and wrapped her in a tight embrace. She clutched at his back, burying her face in his chest and fighting back a fresh round of tears. The past five minutes had thrown more emotional upheavals at her than the last decade. But she found serenity in the comfort of his arms. He murmured words into her hair, stroking her cheeks and curls, then he tipped her face up for a kiss.

Betty smiled up at Everett, but her joy dimmed on a thought. "Why don't I want to kill you? If that's the command I was given and I'm helpless to ignore it, why am I not trying to choke you again?"

"Back at the library, right before Adam tasered you, I gave you the command that you never had to obey the command again." Regret crept into Everett's expression and he chuffed

Betty's arms to warm them. "Sweetheart, I can remove the wiring for the override command. But it would be a surgical procedure. And I won't do it unless you are okay with it."

Her blood iced over at the thought of surgery. "Why would you need to remove it? Your command worked."

"For now. But what's to say someone else won't override my override?" He frowned. "Removing it completely is the only way to be sure."

"And you can do this?"

He nodded, determination setting his expression. "Dr. Farrow will help with the surgical aspect. He's worked with cyborgs since the beginning. Nothing is guaranteed when someone pokes around the CPU part of the brain, but it's a straightforward procedure, and my working knowledge of the system is better than most."

"So, there's a chance I could sustain a brain injury. Or my CPU might be compromised, which would affect my cybernetic functions." Betty placed her hands on his chest, his pectorals flexing deliciously beneath her touch. Everett nodded, not a bit happy about either possibility she listed. "But if it works, I get complete autonomy of my body and my mind. I'll be completely free from my work as a spy."

Again, he nodded, a glint of hope in his eyes. She cupped his face. "Which means I'd be free to love you. I'd risk anything for that. Everett, please do the surgery."

Betty pulled him in for a deep, desperate kiss.

By the time they came up for air, Betty had wrapped her legs around Everett's hips, his erection pressed against her thigh through the crinoline layers of her skirt. Adam had covered his eyes and was shaking his head, and Eve ineffectively hid her triumphant smile behind her hand as she giggled. "Lord, save us from horny cyborgs."

Chapter Eighteen

"Everett, do you need a scalpel or a screwdriver?"

Doc Farrow's voice pulled Everett back to the surgery at hand. Betty lay face-down on the operating table, the massage-table face cradle allowing her neck to be flat and fully exposed, but her ample breasts put the rest of her body in an awkward position. More straps immobilized her arms and legs, again for everyone's safety. Doc had anesthetized the incision area of her neck, but Betty was otherwise awake to give instant feedback on their progress. They'd had to shave a patch of her hair above the CPU access panel, and she had joked she might switch her style from pinup to punk rock as a result.

Everett didn't find any humor in this situation.

Betty must have sensed his unease. Her voice was muffled from the padding which cushioned and secured her head, but her sunshine tone reached his ears as if she stood beside him. "Everett dear, let's not dawdle. It's late and I'm ready to get out of my party dress."

Doc chuckled. Everett swallowed. "I'm getting to it, sweetheart. I'm just not used to seeing my systems... in their intended environment."

Doc chuckled again and leaned closer to Betty as if to share a secret. "Cut him a bit of slack, my dear. He's unnerved by the blood."

Betty chuckled as well.

Doc joked, but there wasn't any blood to be squeamish about. The incision line cut through the scars from when Betty had carved out her own modem, so there had been only a thin trickle of blood. Everett stared past the loose flap of her neck tissue and silicone access panel Doc had secured open, and into the mass of twisted wires, connectors, cache, buses, memory ports, and solder points comprising the bulk of her motherboard. The computer he'd created in powerful miniature from cutting-edge organic-compatible and flexible materials that did not rust or break, yet which held geobytes of data and processed it all faster than a brain synapse. Unlike alpha-phase cyborgs who sported dry internal cases, Beta-phases like Betty had cases filled with thick globs of synthetic lubricant. It coated everything, making it a viscous environment to emulate the body's natural internal state and act as a natural coolant. Essentially, he stared into the guts of his creation.

Neither the view nor the bit of blood from the incision stalled his hands. What made him hesitate was the weight of the knowledge Betty trusted him not to fuck this up.

All he had to do was reach in with the surgical forceps, clip the correct wire at its solder points, and remove the appropriate ROM nodule from her CPU. So familiar with the working of his own creation, he could do it with his eyes closed like a soldier could field-strip a rifle blindfolded. But Everett would have a magnifying surgical camera to use for accuracy. Just in case.

Because he couldn't fuck this up.

Everett laughed, but it held no humor. He'd never before questioned his ability to succeed where cybernetics were concerned. Yet this one basic task had him second-guessing his skill. Why had all his brash confidence evaporated? Simple answer: the stakes were higher than they'd ever been for him. Succeed, and he could live happily-ever-after with Betty. Fail, and she could be irreparably damaged. He'd carry that guilt for the rest of his life.

The slightest, microscopic flinch, and he could lose the woman he loved.

"They don't break, you know." Doc patted him on the shoulder. He wasn't much older than Everett, but his shock of white hair, stout figure, and rimless glasses aged him more than his years. "Humans are pretty tough individuals, and those who become cyborgs are especially resilient. She'll be fine."

Everett nodded in agreement, but couldn't stop the worry that Betty could be broken by his incompetence. But neither could he relinquish the responsibility of this procedure to anyone else. They wouldn't know what to look for. They'd shred her CPU like a tornado. Her tangle of scarlet curls splayed across the headrest. He wanted those same curls similarly splayed across his pillows for the remainder of their days. Everett was the only one with the knowledge to guarantee success. He was the only one who could secure the future with Betty he envisioned.

"Betty, I know I said a few days was too soon to feel this way." Everett's voice echoed in the sterile lab-slash-operating room, amplified so everyone heard. He didn't glance to see their expressions, caring only that Betty knew without a doubt what was in his heart. "But I love you."

She stiffened. After several heartbeats during which he was certain she'd laugh at him, she relaxed. Her soft chuckle reached his ears the same time as the watery *plips* of tears hitting the tile floor beneath her. "Then let's get this procedure over with so you can say that to my face and I can say mine to yours." There was no sadness in her voice, only joy. "Because no romance novel lets the protagonist declare his love to the woman's backside."

Everett glanced at her bottom half, draped in a white surgical blanket which emphasized the curves her clothes only hinted at.

A grunt of appreciation escaped his lips. "Well, I do love your backside, too."

Everyone chuckled. Including Everett.

Like flipping a switch, the tension in the room dispersed. Its presence not even obvious until its absence was so noticeable. Everett's own tension drained, replaced with his typical confidence. Maybe more confidence, because Betty said she had her own declaration of love to give. Those could be hollow words to inspire him to success, but the hope she truly loved him in return bolstered his ego more than any personal or professional accomplishment ever had.

He wouldn't fuck up.

Easing the three slender instruments through her access port, his gaze was glued to the camera screen, watching the cautious progression toward his destination. Doc monitored the steady rhythm of Betty's heartbeat and brain function. Eve and Adam stood at a distance, ready to taze Betty again in the event she went rogue. *Rogue.* Such a misnomer, that word. All the world thought cyborgs randomly lost control of themselves and went on destructive killing sprees, like the one who'd ravaged a Chicago rush hour. Over the years, Everett had berated himself endlessly, racking his brain to figure out what mistake he'd made, what system weakness he'd disregarded that could possibly cause such a colossal malfunction that a cyborg would go *rogue.*

As Doc and his gang had recently discovered, that malfunction wasn't even a malfunction. Someone was downloading command codes via cybernetic modems. Someone was targeting specific cyborgs to act out for specific reasons. Had they targeted Everett during that rush hour standoff? Was Everett supposed to have died in an apparent display of irony at the hands of his own creation?

Who would do such a thing? And more importantly, why would Hawks want him dead?

Everett practically snorted. The answer was obvious. With him out of the way, Hawks could do whatever he wanted with cybernetics. He could declare an end to cybernetics research, and then mold the industry into his own army of superhuman soldiers following orders without question because their ability to think for themselves and disobey direct orders had been stripped away. All without society being aware it was happening.

The more Everett learned about Hawks—the more his eyes were opened to the kind of megalomaniacal tyrant the man was —the more Everett resented his own part in helping Hawks reach his goals. His own shortsightedness, looking no further than the dollar signs. What had begun as a way to serve humanity, and yes make money doing it, had turned into a nightmare for everyone except Richard Hawks.

Everett frowned. *What would the neighbors think?*

Millimeter by millimeter, his instruments crept through the jungle of Betty's cybernetics, ever closer to the correct wire bundle, his heart pounding a steady countdown like a Hollywood bomb scene. He didn't rush. To rush could set off the bomb that was Betty. To keep them all safe, he had to be steadfast. He had to be certain. When he reached the hair-width wire, he paused.

"You doing okay, sweetheart?"

Betty murmured her assent. "I might have to pee soon."

Doc glanced at him. "I can put a catheter in, but it will jostle her. And her panel is already open."

Everett shook his head. "This should only take a few more minutes. Sweetheart, I'm going to wiggle the wire. Let us know if it affects you."

He carefully separated the wire from its bundle and grasped it with the forceps. A slight twist tugged it. She gasped, her words slurring. "I juss got tunnel vision."

"Eve, would you look to see if she's spacing out?"

Eve scurried under the table, tucking her long legs under as

Everett twisted the wire more. "Betty, it's Eve. Focus on me, okay? Look at me. Can you see me?"

Betty said nothing. Eve peeked out from under the table. "Everett, her eyes are unfocused. And she'd not responding to her name."

A terrifying purgatory state of in between, the moment that must happen right after the command code and right before the command. He'd seen her experience it. Even if he had to pull out her cybernetics one wire at a time, she'd never have to suffer it again. This was his silent vow.

He stopped twisting the wire and nodded at Eve. "That's when she's most susceptible to external orders. Yell if she gets to that state again."

She shot him a thumbs-up and resumed her awkward post beneath Betty without complaint. Everett inhaled a bracing breath, mustering the courage to snip the wire. In his lab, he always had the luxury of trial and error to perfect his systems. Here, his actions were final. There would be no chance for repair if he made a mistake.

One final inhale and he held it. Everett snipped the wire at the solder point. It was done. He exhaled, his heart racing, his fingers trembling, his nerves more frazzled than during his first kiss. "You doing okay sweetheart?"

"Still have to pee."

"Oh yeah? What would the neighbors think?"

She snorted. "Who cares what the neighbors would think? I'm sure they have bodily functions, too."

Adam snorted. "Everett, you sure you didn't accidently turn the *Sass* dial up to eleven?"

Everett brushed a hand along the back of her head. What he had to say should prove whether the procedure had been a success. He cleared his throat and forced his voice to be strong. "Betty, I want you to kill me."

She tried to pull her head up to look at him, but he held it in place with his hand. She still had an open portal in her neck and emptying that lubricant down her back would be bad.

Betty growled. "Everett Dean, after all my efforts to keep you alive, killing you would be rather counterproductive. Wild horses couldn't make me do it."

"Could Richard Hawks make you do it?" Adam piped up, his arms crossed over his chest and standing close enough to intervene swiftly.

"Or an override command?" Doc interjected.

Eve's voice was soft with empathy from beneath the table. "Yeah, Betty. What would the neighbors think?"

No one moved, no one spoke. Barely anyone breathed. Waiting for a sign the procedure had been successful. Or not.

Eve poked her head from under the table, a triumphant smile on her face. "She didn't space out. In fact, she's absolutely pissed."

"Meaning she still might kill you." Adam smirked.

Everett nodded. "As long as it's her own free will to do so."

Doc patted Everett on the shoulder, chuckling. "Oh, you got it bad, son."

Everett chuckled as well, relieved beyond words the procedure had worked. But it wasn't finished. From where he'd snipped the wire, he unwound it from the bundle until it came to the other solder point a few inches away. He snipped the wire at that point and pulled it out of its viscous home, dropping it on the instrument tray. Then he entered once more to pluck out the nodule, so no one could attempt to rewire it. Retreating with the same care as when he first entered, he held the nodule above the tray with the wire, and crushed it with the forceps.

Just to be sure.

Unable to contain his triumphant smile, he turned to Doc. "I think she's good. We can put her back together."

Doc *whooped* and made quick work of her access panel and the flap of skin he'd cut. Eve crawled from under the table and leaned into Adam's arms, relief and joy—and a smidgeon of lust —in their expressions as they held each other. The air of elation cavorting in the room was so potent, Everett nearly missed the soft sniffles coming from under the headrest and the quiet *plips* of teardrops falling to the floor.

Betty was crying. Hopefully happy tears. But the fact she cried at all gripped his heart in a vice. Yeah, he definitely had it bad for her. So bad, he could barely wait for Doc to finish stitching and bandaging the incision before Everett threw off her bonds and folded her into his arms. She buried her face in his chest, her body trembling with each inhale, hiccupping with each exhale.

"Sweetheart, why are you crying?" Everett murmured into her hair and cradled her upper body against his. "Are you sad? Happy? What's going on? How can I help?"

"I don't know." Her voice was muffled against his shirt. She shook her head, then tilted it to the side, drawing in a stuttering breath. "I don't know why or how, but something let loose. Like a flood in my brain. Information. Data. Memories. I'm not sure. There's so much of it, it hurts."

Everett looked at Doc, who stared at Betty with brows furrowed in concern. "Doc, she has no modem, so she's not downloading anything. What could this be?"

"My guess is removing the nodule released data she'd stored." Doc stepped closer and rested a comforting hand her back. "Betty, I know it hurts, but is there anything you recognize? Anything familiar?"

She shook her head, groaning in pain and gripping Everett's shirt, clawing at the skin beneath. He barely felt it, so focused was he on her discomfort. His muscles twitched, ready to open her access panel back up and rip out all her cybernetics. His systems—his pride and joy—were no better than garbage if they made her this miserable. The only thing stalling his action was her desperate hold on him.

"I see..." She groaned again. "I see people. Memories of people." She pressed her face into his chest again, as if afraid to face the truth. But, as much as he wished it were possible, he couldn't help her escape what was in her head. "People I've met. People I—"

She jerked back on a gasp so Everett lost his grip and nearly dropped her. But she'd regained full control and sat upright on the table, her cheeks wet with tears and her eyes wide with shock. "They were my targets."

Goosebumps pebbled her bare arms, whether from the chill of the room or the memories she was reliving, he couldn't tell. He rubbed her arms as fresh tears fell from her eyes, her moan the barren pain of a haunting specter. She gasped and clutched her hands to her chest, her voice a broken whisper. "My targets. I never knew for sure, but had always worried I'd been ordered to sleep with them. Assumed I had."

Sobs quaked her body. Everett wrapped his arms around her, rocking her gently and fighting the desire to march straight to D.C. and beat the living shit out of Hawks for having put her through this hell. But Everett's desire to offer what little comfort he could outweighed everything else. "Shhhh. Sweetheart, it doesn't mean anything. Remember, none of that defines you. It doesn't make *you* who you are."

She pulled away from him to look in his eyes. Her makeup was smeared and streaked. Her hair was tousled and tangled. Her eyes were puffed from crying, her nose red, and a thin trail of snot shot out along one cheekbone. She was the most beautiful woman he'd ever known. She was an angel, having slogged through some of the deepest, darkest infested swamps humanity could place her in and coming out on the other side a kind and hopeful soul.

Betty shook her head as he dipped his to kiss her, her voice thick with emotion but her eyes twinkling and her mouth wide with a beaming smile. "That's just it. I didn't sleep with them. I didn't have sex with my targets. I wasn't that kind of escort."

She cupped Everett's face, laughter bubbling from her throat. "I'm not soiled goods. You didn't fall in love with a whore."

Everett pulled back. His heart wrenched, his blood stilled. She thought he cared about her sexual history? "When did I say any of that mattered to me? When did I say you were soiled or call you a whore?"

The jubilance faded from her face. Her mouth opened and closed like a fish, no words coming out.

He palmed her cheek with one hand and brushed her hair away from her face with the other. "Betty, I hate that my systems made it possible for someone to strip away your control. I hate what you must have suffered, thinking you'd been used like that. But what you did or might have done in the past does not have any influence over my love for you. I love you. I love you for who you are right now. Not what you were, what you might have been, or even what you could be. I want to stand beside you, face the future together with you, and grow with you, because of the woman you are right now."

Fresh tears sprung to her eyes and her mouth open and closed again, no sound coming forth. She swallowed and rested her hands lightly on his chest. "Oh. Um… same. I mean. Uh. I love you, too."

Everett might have laughed at Betty's awkward confession, if she hadn't groaned *so lame* and rolled her eyes before plunking her forehead against his pectoral. Before he could reassure her, three other voices rang out in a smitten *Aaawwwww!*

His arms around her, because he might not ever let her go, he twisted to look at their audience. Doc held a hand to his heart, an inscrutable smile on his face. Adam sported a knowing grin, his arm draped across Eve's shoulders. Eve applauded silently then waved her fingers at her eyes as if to fight forthcoming tears. "That was like a scene from a movie."

"Trust me." Betty sniffed. "The book was better."

Before he could be tempted to kiss her again, Everett grabbed her by the waist and helped her dismount the table. Doc detached the last of the monitor wires then checked her incision. "I know this has been a long day, but why don't we all get comfortable and break bread together?"

"Don't have to ask me twice." Adam licked his lips and rubbed his belly. "Knowing David, he's been simmering his oxtail and poblano stew this whole time."

Eve elbowed him in the gut with a laugh. "Knowing you, you just want to sneak a slice of his tres leches cake."

Adam laughed as he steered her toward the door. "Darlin,' you know you're the dessert I love best."

Chapter Nineteen

Betty sopped up the last of her stew with a chunk of crunchy bread. The rich meat and spices warmed her belly nearly as much as Everett's declaration of love. He loved her. He'd loved her when he'd been told she'd slept with half of the government. He'd loved her even as she'd tried to choke him.

Maybe she was dreaming.

She sat on a couch, having traded her wrinkled dress for a borrowed pair of comfy sweats, leaning against Everett's side while his fingers traced unconscious designs on her shoulder, neck, and in her hair. Doc, Adam, Eve, a man called David, and a retired cyborg police dog name Apollo lounged in similar fashion around a cozy patio setting situated in a bomb shelter several stories below the surface. A bomb shelter with state-of-the-art sleeping rooms, kitchen, living areas, and hydroponic plants tucked in every possible nook and cranny. The arched ceiling forty feet above them was a domed screen of the night sky, stars twinkling and a crescent moon as if they truly relaxed in a verdant backyard. Doc had explained the bunker was originally built by his grandfather, with serious improvements through the years by Doc himself. The result was lusher than the

White River Gardens, more luxurious than a five-star hotel, and more self-contained than a cruise ship. They could survive Armageddon for several years in comfort. Even longer if they were conservative with their toilet paper usage.

End-of-times prep aside, the others relaxed on couches with clean lines and a watery color palate, talking quietly and enjoying the last of David's stew, delicious evidence of his Hispanic culture. Doc and David shared a loveseat, sitting more closely than the couch and male friendship required. They exchanged tender touches and heated glances, their love for each other obvious. Across from them, Eve leaned against Adam in much the same way Betty leaned into Everett. Adam spoon-fed Eve from his bowl while she tore off chunks of bread for him to dip with.

Yep, Betty was dreaming.

Apollo curled up against Eve's legs, his demeanor relaxed but his eyes and ears attuned to the slightest change, no doubt a result of his breed as well as his training. Old habits die hard. Betty knew this fact poignantly. Like Apollo, she couldn't quite relax her guard, even as everyone joked and spoke openly about cyborgs. Too many years spent on the edge of that knife, fearing someone would learn her secret. Scared her handler would find her.

"David, your stew was pretty tasty for a knuckle-dragging hose jockey." Adam teased loudly, smacking his lips for emphasis and rubbing his flat stomach like a pregnant woman.

David laughed, his dark eyes dancing from the good-natured ribbing. "You're welcome to volunteer for a meal shift. But I'm not sure donuts and coffee count."

Adam shrugged. "It would be better than Eve's spaghetti Pad Thai."

"Considering the meager ingredients I found in your bachelor-pad of a house, you're lucky I could make anything edible." Eve huffed as if offended.

Everett leaned his head down and murmured in Betty's ear. "Should I tell them how divine your brownies are?"

He didn't murmur softly enough, and all eyes turned toward her, interest alight in their faces. The sudden attention unnerved. She'd spent too many years being looked at but not seen. Homeless. Escort. Librarian. But never... Betty. And definitely not Luann. Maybe her pinup model clothes and artfully applied makeup, and even her new identity, had been less a style choice and more a sort of costume. A mask meant to keep the world at arms-length so no one would see her for who she really was.

Because who she really was had always disappointed.

"Brownies?" Adam waggled his eyebrows. "I like brownies."

"How are you not fat?" Eve swatted him on the leg on a laugh.

He pulled her in for a tight side hug and placed a loud smooch on her temple. "I'll give you three guesses how I work off all this delicious food."

"I'm very grateful my grandfather had the foresight to make the bedrooms soundproof." Doc sniffed in disdain and cleaned his glasses with his shirt.

Eve tossed a chunk of crust at him with a knowing smile. "Oh, you're one to talk, Doc."

Knowing snickers erupted, followed by friendly conversation as if the six of them were old friends. Well, five of them, at least. As each moment of relaxed companionship passed, Betty grew more tense. She'd lived for decades on her own, fighting and scraping for a living in a harsh world, afraid someone would notice her and take away what little she had. Then she'd chosen to become a cyborg, and the cycle had become even more perilous. She'd never experienced casual camaraderie like what these couples extended without question or contention to Everett and to her.

She waited for the other shoe to drop. Waited for these so-called friends to morph into foes.

"Sweetheart, what's wrong?" Everett chuffed her arm and planted a tender kiss atop her head. "You're as taut as a wire about to snap."

Betty flicked a hand down her thighs, brushing away invisible crumbs or wrinkles that weren't there because she wore sweatpants… apparently, she had her own massive tells. With a sigh, she placed her soup bowl on the coffee table, then addressed the group. "Forgive me, I don't mean to sound ungrateful. But why am I here?"

The others exchanged looks as if confused by her question. The obtuseness flamed her irritation, and she made no effort to swallow it back. "As far as I can tell, the only reason I'm here is because Eve has been trying to lure me into meeting with her for an unknown reason, and you happened to walk into my library minutes after I'd received a kill order which triggered my override command code which hasn't been used in years."

"Thank God they arrived—" Everett began, but Betty put her hand against his lips and pulled away from him, sitting on the edge of the couch, her muscles rigid with the need to fight. Or flee.

She addressed them all, running each face and posture against her database for some subtle expression or telltale stance to prove they had a hidden agenda. Some sign this was all a ruse. Some evidence she wasn't losing it. Because every passing moment in this beautiful oasis with these accepting individuals was another tap at the glass cage she'd erected around her heart as a hollow promise of safety. Everett had already squeezed in through a hairline fracture. One more tap of kindness, and she might very well shatter.

Emotion lodged in her throat. "Honestly, the coincidence of these two events seems strangely convenient. As if you knew the call from Hawks was coming. As if you're all in it together. I know I sound paranoid, but look at it from my perspective. I've lived a nice, quiet life under the radar from everyone until a few days ago when Eve Myer walked into my library. Since then, it's been upended. By nearly all of you."

"They're on our side, sweetheart." Everett laid a hand on her thigh, but she flinched away. His shoulders drooped from the rejection, but the understanding in his tone never left. "They want to take Richard Hawks down and make life better for cyborgs. We can trust them."

"Adam and I are cyborgs, too." David nodded, as if that statement was all the convincing she required. "We understand what you've been through."

"Being cyborgs doesn't make us friends." She shook her head. "It doesn't put us on the same team."

"Actually, Betty. It kinda does." Adam's voice remained warm in the face of her belligerence. "Being a cop automatically put me in a special fraternity with other officers. Same for David and other firefighters. By the sheer fact you underwent cybernetic surgery, you get a free membership into our club. Welcome."

Doc leaned forward, his elbows braced on his knees. "Betty, I was a rehabilitation specialist for post-op first responder cyborgs during the alpha phase. That experience, combined with my medical knowledge, gives me a specialized understanding of what cybernetic individuals such as you suffer." His expression sobered and he glanced at David and Adam. "The physical pain, the emotional trauma, the societal abhorrence and ultimate isolation… I may not have lived it myself, but I've seen it with countless others."

She lifted one eyebrow. "So, I should trust you because you have experience?"

Adam nodded to indicate Doc. "I trust him, Betty. I trust Doc more than I trust myself."

"I trust him with my life." David was serious as a heart attack.

Doc held his hands up. "We're asking you for trust we

haven't earned yet. Please give us time. We're trying to build a…
a rebel alliance, for lack of a better term, to take down Director
Hawks. To build a better life for cybernetic individuals. We need
all the help we can get, which is why Eve reached out to you
through Charlie. We didn't want to alarm you."

David snorted. "Guess we screwed the pooch on that."

"Betty, I trust him." Everett rested his fingertips on her
shoulder. "I trust him enough to let him cut on you to get to your
access panel. That surgery could have gone south any number of
ways. But it didn't."

Betrayal fluttered at the edge of her heart. She understood
why the others would be so devoted to Doc and his cause. But
why Everett?

"You've only known them for half a day." She faced him,
needing his support. Wanting his confirmation. "Why do you
trust them so much?"

He scrubbed his fingers along his jaw, as if contemplating his
answer. Then he slid off the couch to kneel in front of her,
pulling her hands into his, their warmth a reminder of the home
she'd always wanted. The home she'd never had.

He gazed directly into her eyes, solemn like he was swearing
a blood oath. "Betty, I trust them because my head is telling me
not to. I can think of a hundred logical reasons why I shouldn't.
For why I should turn this whole operation in to the authorities.
But I can only think of two reasons why I should side with them:
One, my heart is telling me to. And two, there's no money to be
made doing it. Those reasons contradict the decision-making
process that has ruled my entire adult life. And that's got to
count for something."

"That's all?" Her head screamed a litany of arguments to
counter his explanation. But her heart was quiet, having already
embraced his reasons as her own. "You settled on a new course
in life based entirely on not making decisions the way you
always have before?"

Could the answer be so simple? Was life ever that simple?

"Pretty much." Everett shrugged, looking sheepish. "I might be a cybernetic genius, but otherwise I'm a pretty simple man. Trusting my head and my pocketbook never gained me any friends or lovers I could truly be myself with. So trusting my heart instead seems a better option. Just like I've trusted my heart where you are concerned."

She leaned closer, lips quivering, and whispered. "I'm terrified. What if it's the wrong decision?"

He cupped her cheeks. "So am I. But have any of our decisions in the past been so very stellar?" When she shook her head, he brushed his lips against hers. "Maybe this one isn't any smarter. But if we're together, at least we won't be lonely."

All the fight whooshed out of her like air escaping a balloon. She was tired of struggling alone. Tired of always looking over her shoulder and keeping to herself. Tired of hearing the hate and vitriol and having to bite her tongue. Tired of watching her every word for fear someone would look at her askance. Trusting this group might not be the wisest decision. But as Everett had pointed out, it couldn't be any worse than any of the others she'd made in her life. And she wouldn't be alone.

She leaned into Everett's arms and he swooped her into them and sat back on the couch, settling her onto his lap. She rested her head in the crook of his neck and looked around. The others hadn't moved, having witnessed Everett's explanation and Betty's capitulation with varying expressions of awe and understanding. Each of them had lives irrevocably changed by cybernetics and the manipulations of a certain Richard Hawks. If they banded together to go up against everyone using cyborgs for personal gain, who could say what the outcome would be like? But even if their story didn't have a happy ending, Betty wanted a hand in writing it. Excitement fluttered in her chest like a butterfly with new wings.

"You're right, Everett. It doesn't make any sense to trust

them. Not after only knowing them a couple hours like I have." Betty rested her hand against his heart and lifted her head back to look him in the eyes. "But I fell in love with you after only a couple days. I guess time doesn't matter when it's right."

His smile was brighter than the sun, and he leaned to kiss her, but someone cleared their throat, stemming the rising arousal. David's no-nonsense voice pierced through their lust. "If you two start doing it here, I'm hosing you down."

Eve threw a chunk of bread at David. "Oh, like *you're* one to talk!"

Betty wrapped her arms tighter around Everett's neck and focused her attention on Doc. "Well, if I'm joining this rebel alliance, I'll need access to a computer." She waved her fingerjack in the air and slanted him a mischievous grin. "During my spy days, it seems I collected enough intel to take down a government. I didn't know this until today, but instead of dumping that data once it was uploaded to Hawks, I saved it to an auxiliary memory core."

She turned her gaze to Everett as the collective gasp settled. "Would you like to know his overseas bank account numbers?"

Epilogue

"Charlie! It's good to see you again." Luann looked up from basket of hydroponic tomatoes she harvested from the sunlight-simulated HydroFoods ground-level warehouse to greet the familiar face. Doc had created the front company, located in the former Park 100 industrial area, to explain away his bunker's massive energy and water consumption. The company was truly a hidden gem. Tucked amid abandoned warehouses in a forgotten part of Indianapolis, HydroFoods Inc. was a cutting-edge source of food that Doc donated to the indigent population in the area.

Not unlike the lunches she had offered to homeless individuals around the library. Except on a much larger scale. When she'd had made the comparison to Eve, the other woman had elbowed her and winked. "Well Done. You're a Rebel now." Then she'd offered her own working theory that Doc's *rebel alliance* was more than a fledgling idea, and that many of the transient individuals he fed were members of his covert army.

Charlie's eye widened in shock at seeing Luann. Then his dirt-stained face creased in a smile.

She set her basket down and, out of habit, brushed a hand down the front of her well-worn jeans which she'd grabbed from Doc's prepper stash of clothing. Her pinup dresses had been traded for more casual—and comfortable—fare, partially because no one had thought to pack her a suitcase when they'd tasered her to save Everett. But mostly because she didn't need to hide behind those costumes any more. Less than a week spent with Doc and the gang in his fancy bunker, and she knew without a doubt this was her family. Her safe place. Her home.

She smiled at Charlie. "Surprised that I'm here?"

"Not really." He shrugged, the expression beneath his beard just shy of sheepish. "But I didn't expect you to be so… relaxed."

She twined her fingers together. Her previous interaction with Charlie hadn't been very relaxed. "I owe you an apology for how I reacted the last time I saw you."

"No apology needed, Miss B." He shook his head, his tangled strands of hair swaying. "I woulda reacted the same, if it'd been me."

"Charlie, please call me Luann. It's my real name." She waved to indicate the warehouse, and the hidden stories of Doc's *Batcave* beneath it. "No need for me to hide any more, is there?"

"Not 'round these folks, no." He smiled at her, then dropped his gaze to the ground and scuffed a worn shoe on the concrete floor. "I know you're all busy. But I'd like to chat with Doc if he's around."

Luann wasn't certain how to answer that. If this was truly Doc's rebel alliance, was Charlie a part of it? Was she allowed to allow anyone inside the bunker? She and Everett called the shelter *home*, but there was still so much for her to learn. She didn't want to overstep.

Eve moseyed up from the other side of the tomato row. "What's going on, Charlie? Got a message to give to Doc?"

His shoulders drooped and he shrugged, his hands shoved in his pants pockets. "I'd prefer to give it to him personally, Miss Eve."

Eve looked at Luann for a moment before claiming her tomato basket and nodding toward the hidden stairwell in the far corner. "I think he's in the lab with Everett."

With Eve's permission, Luann escorted Charlie down a few flights of stairs to the spacious laboratory area which also functioned as a surgical area and had recently held her captive. Adam referred to it as the repair shop, but it looked more like an android factory to her. Brightly lit with bins and walls of drawers spilling over with cybernetic materials. Arms, legs, eyes, spools of wires, and all manner of computer parts.

This was the room she'd first met Adam and Doc. The room where her override command had been disabled. The room where Everett had first professed his love.

What had initially been a hostage situation had ended with small victories and had begun a new family dynamic she still traversed with the occasional awkwardness. But like Everett had said, at least they weren't alone any more.

She ushered Charlie in through the hermetic door which slid open with a quiet *snick*. Everett and Doc stood to the side, deep in conversation, holding what looked like a thick silicone balloon and stretching it any number of ways. Their focus so intent, they didn't even hear Luann and Charlie as they padded softly toward them. Rather than risk giving either a heart attack, she spoke as they approached. "Is it someone's birthday? Are we blowing up balloons?"

Both men looked up, Doc with gleeful surprise on his face and Everett with the much softer look of a man deeply in love. With her. Everett loved her. She wore the fact like a new pair of shoes to break in; still a little stiff and uncertain, but with the potential to be amazing. Until then, she would gladly suffer the jumble of nerves and ill-timed arousal which so often happened around him. Like they did now.

"Luann, my dear." Doc waved her forward and indicated the silicone bag. "It's funny you should mention birthdays. Everett and I were discussing an innovation related to that."

She shrugged. "Not sure how birthdays can be improved."

"I—well, *we*—" Everett looked at a loss for words, but never broke his gaze with hers. "We were talking cybernetic uteruses. My Preditech staff had tossed around the possibility a few years ago, but Hawks pretty much squelched the idea then. Doc and I were discussing the details."

She twined her hands at her belly and spoke with hesitation, not sure why her input would be of value in that discussion, or even how she felt about the idea. "I'm sure there are many women who might be interested in it."

Everett nodded with enthusiasm, as if she'd handed him a plate of brownies. "Yes, women who have had problems carrying a baby to term. Or women who… suffer fibromyalgia. Or women who can't conceive." His voice softened and she felt his gaze like a hug. "Or women who had their uteruses removed, due to cancer or… other reasons."

She'd had hers removed to be a cyborg spy. But Everett could give her a new one? He could create a cyborg uterus so she could try for another baby? Her hands instinctively spread across her belly, the emptiness there as emotional as it was physical. She couldn't bring back the baby she'd lost, but with Everett's help, she could have a second chance.

Did he want a child as well?

He stepped forward and brushed away the tears streaming down her cheek. When had she begun crying? "Luann, you don't have to say *yes*. And you don't have to answer today, or even anytime soon. Just know it's a possibility." He wrapped his arms around her and rested his cheek atop her head. This was how they drifted to sleep every night, in each other's embrace as if they could handle anything as long as they were together.

"Even with a working uterus, hasn't that ship already sailed for me?" She murmured against his chest. "Aren't I too old?"

Doc cleared his throat. "Technically we don't know the answer to that. In my experience, cybernetics makes the human body stronger. And there seems some evidence it slows the aging process." He speared a hand through his white hair as if to illustrate his point. "It would be uncharted territory, but not impossible."

She pulled back to look up at Everett. "Is this something you would want? It can't be my decision, because I can't raise a child alone."

"I would want this. With you. And I think the others could be talked into babysitting on occasion." Everett placed a gentle kiss on the tip of her nose, then slanted Doc a mischievous grin. Doc nodded his head so vigorously, his shock of hair bounced, his expression like a child getting a new puppy.

She laughed and squeezed Everett, her heart dancing with love and hope, like when she finished reading a romance novel. No, her life wasn't a horror story or political thriller… it was a romance. A *second chance former bad boy billionaire forced proximity not-so-secret baby political intrigue rom-com* romance… Not a trope everyone would be interested in, but as long as it ended with a happily-ever-after, Luann couldn't wait to begin it.

A contented sigh escaped her lips. "Okay you two, I promise I'll think about the baby thing. But I came here because Charlie wants a word with Doc."

Doc patted the young man on the shoulder. "What do you need, my boy?"

"Thought you might want to know." Charlie drew in a deep breath, an act which straightened his affected slouch and added a few inches to his height. "I recently heard from my sister."

"The one who works in D.C.?" Doc clarified.

"I never told ya, but she works for the DCO." Charlie nodded, then looked right in Doc's eyes. "And she's got intel that will bring it all down."

About the Author

Ava Cuvay is an award-winning, bestselling author who writes out of this world Sci-fi Romance featuring sassy heroines, gutsy heroes, passion, adventure, and an alcoholic beverage or two... often set in a galaxy far, far away. She resides in central Indiana with her own scruffy-looking nerfherder, teens who don't realize just how cool she is, and two kitties that make her laugh. She believes life is too short to bother with negative people, everything is better with Champagne, and Han Solo shot first.

Sign up for an Exclusive Bonus Scene and More Book News!

Join my newsletter for an exclusive bonus scene, freebies, Advanced Reader Copy opportunities, and fun info! https://drinkingthestarspressllc.eo.page/kxdnn

Stalk Me!

Check me out and follow me on your preferred platform:

Website for a complete listing of her books: AvaCuvay.com

Facebook Page: AvaCuvayAuthor

Goodreads Page: https://www.goodreads.com/author/show/15051407.Ava_Cuvay

BookBub: https://www.bookbub.com/authors/ava-cuvay

Amazon Author Page: https://www.amazon.com/Ava-Cuvay/e/B01E5OIZ0I/

Please Leave a Review!

Book reviews are one of the few ways we authors receive feedback from our readers. And we hunger for it! Please take a few minutes and leave a review this book. Thank you!

"Tin Soldier" Sneak Peek

"Audra Muir has gone AWHOL." The three-star Lieutenant General seated behind his overcompensating-for-something-sized desk announced in a booming voice, as if he issued orders in the middle of a battlefield. Not that he'd ever seen active combat. Gage Austin would bet his measly Staff Sergeant's pension on that fact.

Still, Lt. General JR Higgenbotham outranked him by a lifetime even though they were only a few years apart in age. Gage wasn't about to relax his stance or question why the Lt. General had called him on the carpet when Gage wasn't even part of Higgenbotham's department.

The late morning sun slanting through the executive office window cast Higgenbotham in a spotlight and glinted off his chest brass like twinkle lights on the Christmas tree. But nothing about this meeting was festive. Higgenbotham leaned forward on his elbows, spearing Gage with a withering glower. "Care to enlighten me on where my secretary is, Staff Sergeant?"

Gage glanced over at his boss, Master Sergeant Aquiles Sohl, who looked as confused as he felt, and back to Higgenbotham. "Wh-why would I know where Ms. Muir is, Sir?"

He had also been wondering where Audra was these past several weeks. They weren't anything to one another, but he sure liked looking at her as they passed in the halls. She was a beautiful woman. A cherubic heart-shaped face, dainty sky-sloped nose, eyes the color of the Caribbean's warm waters, and willful blonde curls threaded with the occasional silver. He would love to be more than a passing acquaintance with her.

But he was a cyborg. A retired Army vet with enhanced cybernetic systems and a machine gun leg no one here at the Pentagon knew about because that detail might incite a public panic. Which meant *passing acquaintance* was all he and Audra could ever be to one another. He was smart enough to keep this in mind when they made small talk at the elevators or wound up in the same line at the food court. And she was beguiling enough she didn't need to pursue a washed-up veteran like him who eked out his remaining days in a dead-end desk job.

Yet there had been that one morning…

"You have the audacity to ask *why* you should know where she is?" Higgenbotham practically growled. "Because you're fucking her!"

The animosity in Higgenbotham's voice echoed in the room and set Gage back on his heels. Sohl also flinched, but responded. "Lieutenant General Higgenbotham, Sir, I can assure you Staff Sergeant—"

"Everyone knows you two are going at it like rabbits." Higgenbotham interrupted, disgust creeping into his tone, his glare never leaving Gage. Was the thought of him in a physical relationship with Audra that offensive? "And the security records prove it."

Damn. If Higgenbotham had watched the security vids, he'd seen what should have been a private interlude between Gage and Audra. He stared straight ahead, not meeting Higgenbotham's gaze to see his reaction to the truth. "Not like rabbits, Sir. That's quite an exaggeration. But we did have one impromptu tryst."

That morning encounter had occurred in the boardroom adjoining Higgenbotham's office. Gage and Audra had desecrated the massive conference table with their naked bodies and a variety of bodily fluids. It had been her idea. It had been amazing. It had been exactly the positive human interaction he'd needed on a particularly shitty morning following years of shitty mornings here at the defense headquarters of the country he'd sacrificed a quarter of his body and his happiness to defend.

Higgenbotham and the rest of the Pentagon staff might scorn them for what they'd done and where. But Gage couldn't muster even a gram of regret for the one rendezvous he'd had with Audra. She had acted as if she felt the same.

So why did she disappear?

The voice in his mind mirrored his concerns, but it wasn't his voice. Gage blinked at the weird sensation of someone else in his head. Was he finally about to snap and go rogue, like other cyborgs had done before? Like all of society was afraid might happen at any given moment, thus spurring their distrust of his kind?

Why don't you go find her?

Again that strange voice, but a question he'd asked himself countless times over the past weeks since their romp in Higgenbotham's boardroom. Gage usually saw Audra several times a day during the normal course of his menial duties. But he'd only seen her a few times the rest of that week. And then not at all since. He shouldn't worry about it. One quick, no-strings-attached fuck didn't mean anything. It certainly didn't beholden him to her care and safety, nor her to keeping him informed of her whereabouts. But hers had been the only friendly face in this place. Even after the sex, they'd exchanged only awkward small talk in passing, but it was more interaction than he had with most people, and more than he should have with any one person. Becoming a cyborg had killed his career, his personal life, and any hopes for a sex life with the exception of his daily pat-down by the Pentagon security officers.

"You say you two fucked only one time, but that's most meaningful contact anyone at the Pentagon has had with her."

Gage frowned at this obviously falsehood. Audra was the friendliest person he'd ever known. In the years he'd observed her from a relative distance, she always had a bright smile and welcome greeting for everyone. Quick to engage in conversation, a ready laugh and a kind word on her tongue, she captivated all within her circle.

Sohl cleared his throat. "Lieutenant General, forgive my surprise that you would consider the… uh… interaction… my Staff Sergeant had with Ms. Muir as more meaningful than the working relationship you surely had with her. After all, she was your secretary for several years, wasn't she?"

Higgenbotham's gaze ping-ponged between the two men, looking like he'd rather chew glass than utter his next gruff words. "I'm a firm believer that an employee should leave their personal life at home. She was proficient in her work duties, and professional in her demeanor. That was all I cared about."

Audra deserved better than to work for a man whose greatest compliments were *professional* and *proficient.* The Pentagon environment was fast-paced and cutthroat, but most supervisors treated their subordinates like actual humans. Even Sohl encouraged Gage to have a work-life balance, as if that was possible.

"But her unexpected absence is affecting the department's workload and deadlines." Higgenbotham hurried to add, as if he could compensate for his tepid praise of his secretary by blaming her for his department's failures. "We have vital military contracts that need to be vetted and signed, and she is the only one with that information. But she's MIA."

Higgenbotham threw his hands up in a sign of defeat, or as a declaration of his own innocence in this debacle. Either way one interpreted the move, it defied both the Army's motto and the soldier's creed which should define his life. Gage's hands fisted, so he clasped them behind his back under the pretense of adjusting his stance. The asshole didn't deserve an employee like Audra.

You should offer to search for Audra.

The strange voice in his head didn't make sense. Tracking down truant employees was not in his job description or his pay grade.

Higgenbotham's eyes lit up and he sat back in his chair as if he'd thought of the perfect solution to his dilemma. Gage held his breath; if the past five minutes were any indication, Higgenbotham's idea would be a doozy.

"Staff Sergeant Austin, why don't you track Audra Muir down?"

Gage nearly choked. The voice in his head certainly wasn't Higgenbotham's, so why the similar suggestions? Sohl sputtered. "Sir, Staff Sergeant Austin's responsibilities are strictly limited to building operations, not staff. He doesn't have the skills or the—"

"He was an Explosive Ordnance Disposal NCO, wasn't he?" Higgenbotham looked at Sohl like he was stupid. Then he turned that look to Gage. "Well, weren't you?"

"Yes, Lieutenant General. But that was nearly a decade ago, and Ms. Muir is a human being not a bomb—"

"It's settled." Higgenbotham nodded and planted his palms on the desk like a king making a decree that would be followed without question. "Master Sergeant, you'll make Staff Sergeant Austin available to search and return my secretary to me in an expeditious timeframe."

Higgenbotham continued, but Gage had stopped listening, his heart pounding in his ears. Yes, he'd love to see Audra again, but how the hell was he going to find a woman who obviously didn't want to be found ijust because her boss this desperate to get her back?

You're happy with the assignment. You want *to search for Audra.*

Damn that strange voice in his head. How could he listen to the growing argument between Higgenbotham and Sohl with that voice saying those words in his head? Yes, he wanted to know Audra was alive and safe, but it wasn't his place to hunt her down like he was a bloodhound and she an escaped criminal. But what if she was in trouble? What if something bad had happened to her? Maybe she'd been hurt. Maybe she'd been abducted. Maybe she was somewhere wishing someone would come save her, and here he stood trying to avoid the responsibility.

He'd scoffed at Higgenbotham, but Gage's own reactions defied his noncommissioned officer creed and the Army Motto. *This we'll defend.* Saving Audra would uphold the morals by which he'd lived his life. It was the right thing to do.

You'll search for her. Tell them you'll do it.

"I'll do it." Gage blurted, effectively silencing Higgenbotham and Sohl in the middle of their loud argument. The two men both stared at him, Sohl shocked and Higgenbotham smug with self-satisfaction.

Maybe it was the prospect of seeing her again. Maybe it was the thought of doing something more meaningful than processing requisition forms for new lightbulbs and toilet paper. For the first time since he'd become a cyborg and had been shuffled to his desk jockey job here, a glimmer of hope and excitement flickered in his chest.

Gage cleared his throat. "I'll search for and find Audra Muir."

Find "Tin Soldier" are your favorite online retailer: **https://books2read.com/u/brXKkW**